God Bless America: Stories by Some Guy in the Joint

Proceeds from the sale of this book will be used to remedy a miscarriage of justice.

God Bless America: Stories by Some Guy in the Joint

Short fiction about life
inside and outside the walls
to benefit the
Phillip Lippert Defense Fund

Phillip Lippert

Published by the
Phillip Lippert Defense Fund
Adrian, Michigan

These stories were originally written for the amusement of the author's beloved godmother. They have been collected and published here to benefit the Phillip Lippert Defense Fund in hopes of finally seeing justice done on his behalf.

God Bless America: Stories by Some Guy in the Joint

Copyright © 2000 Phillip Lippert

Published by The Phillip Lippert Defense Fund, P.O. Box 132, Adrian, Michigan 49221

Cover and interior design by Lee Lewis, words+design, 888-883-8347

Manufactured in the United States of America

Additional copies may be ordered by sending $13.00, check or money order, to:
The Phillip Lippert Defense Fund
P.O. Box 132
Adrian, Michigan 49221
Visit our website at www.phillip-lippert.com

ISBN 0-9704052-0-0

Cataloging-in-Publication Data
Lippert, Phillip.
     God Bless America : stories by some guy in the joint :
     short fiction about life inside and outside the walls
     to benefit the Phillip Lippert Defense Fund / Phillip
     Lippert -- 1st ed.
     p. cm.

     1. Prisoners--Fiction. 2. Prisons--Fiction.
     3. Texas--Fiction. I. Title

PS3562.I582G64 2000   813.6
          QBI00-901372

Table of Contents

Injustice anywhere is a threat to
justice everywhere.

—Martin Luther King, Jr.

DEDICATION

A wise man once observed that in the land of the blind, a one-eyed man is king. To the world at large, the past three decades of my life would seem to be a sad and pitiful existence. In the land I presently inhabit, though, I'm like the man blessed with one good eye in the midst of the blind masses. Among the wretched, forsaken, and forgotten, I have been blessed with a family who has stood beside me through more than life ever prepared them for—even through the hardest years when I was too ornery and/or depressed to be endured. My parents and sisters still set a place for me at Christmas dinner and leave a lit candle in the window every New Year's Eve. They've always been available with whatever aid and comfort would help ease the burden. Even after shattering the peace and dignity of the small hometown we shared, I still hear from old classmates from high school and receive cards and letters from strangers who feel moved to send their warm thoughts and good wishes. I have been remembered in the prayers of a dying nun and grieved for by people so decent it shames me. I shudder at the thought of what these years would have been without that support, and I have only to look around me to be reminded how blessed I have been.

Opportunities to express heartfelt thanks are rare, and such expressions always seem inadequate. At this point, however, my thanks are all I have to offer. In addition to my parents, I am particularly indebted to my brother Roger, my sisters Kathy, Denise, and Jennifer; Margaret Ann Bloss, a friend and counselor since she was my third-grade Sunday School teacher; and Daniel Raymond Heil. Thank you to the Texans who made that part of my life a cherished memory: Barbara and Eddie Rogers in Brenham, Sharon in Dallas, Annie and Letitia in Austin. Thank you to those many people who wrote the parole board and the governor on my behalf.

Thanks to Lee Lewis, without whose invaluable input and expertise this project would never have left the ground.

Thanks to Roger Lee Brower, for literally hundreds of hours of legal research and strategy, refusing any payment where others had demanded it.

Huge thanks and great affection to Sister Patricia Schnapp, RSM: teacher, mentor, taskmaster, friend. I write because she won't have it any other way.

And with my deepest respect for her incredible fortitude, special thanks to Bridget Ann Hart.

—Phillip Lippert, #128058
Ionia Maximum Facility
1576 Bluewater Highway
Ionia, Michigan 48846

INTRODUCTION

A number of events in recent years have provided a shocking eye-opener for many Americans who thought their system of justice worked just as it is taught in high school civics class. Televised trials of the rich and famous have provided insight into the unique brand of justice available to the privileged. Numerous accounts of police and judicial corruption resulting in horrendous miscarriages of justice have been exposed.

Revealed in recent examinations of death penalty cases is a system where it is commonplace for prosecutors to say and do anything necessary to get a conviction, and defense attorneys who afford their clients no defense and sometimes actually collude with the prosecution. Even some of the most conservative and no-nonsense voices of our time are now conceding that the system is broken. Until it can be repaired overall, individual instances of injustice can, and must, be addressed one case at a time. Mahatma Gandhi once said that the first step in righting a wrong is exposing it to the light of day. The following synopsis of the case of Phillip Lippert is a first step to bring this particular case of manifest injustice to light.

—✺—

On November 19, 1970, Alonzo Hart, Jr., 42, was found murdered outside his home in rural Gratiot County, Michigan. Six weeks later,

3

police arrested William J. Pribble, a 28-year-old ex-Marine. Pribble immediately confessed to committing the murder. He had been paid $100 by the victim's widow, Sarah Jane, 27, with another $2,000 promised from her husband's life insurance policy. Pribble also told police that, on the night of the murder, he was accompanied by Phillip Lippert, a 17-year-old high school senior. Based on information provided by Pribble, Lippert and Mrs. Hart were arrested two days before Christmas, 1970.

The series of events that unfolded from that point forward are so bizarre and convoluted that, if presented as fiction, they would be dismissed as absurd. Ithaca, Michigan, during the time at issue was a small, isolated community very much owned and operated by an "old boy network." Following a series of legal maneuvers that left observers flabbergasted, all charges against the victim's widow were dismissed and she was awarded full payment of her murdered husband's life insurance benefits. At the end of nearly thirty years, it remains a topic of local discussion.

Gratiot County prosecutors issued two warrants for Phillip Lippert's arrest. The first charged him with first degree murder and included the notation that conviction on this charge would be punished by a mandatory sentence of life imprisonment in solitary confinement at hard labor. The second warrant charged Lippert with second degree murder, punishable by imprisonment for any number of years up to and including life, at the discretion of the court.

It must be noted that there is no such thing as being sentenced to a prison term in solitary confinement. There is no such thing in Michigan as being sentenced to hard labor. Most importantly, there is no such thing as being convicted of two degrees of the same crime simultaneously. Overcharging in this manner to coerce a guilty plea is a ploy referred to as "multiplicity of charges." This method has been discredited by the United States Supreme Court and is grossly illegal in all state and federal jurisdictions.

Following his arrest, Lippert's parents hired a local law firm to represent their son and protect his legal rights. In this case, the defendant was a teenage first offender ignorant of the system and dependent upon the integrity of the court and his legal counsel. In both instances, he was let down. In their first consultation, the attorneys set about convincing

4

their young client that, under Michigan law, he was subject to be convicted of *both* of the charges filed against him and that the police had an "air-tight" case. They advised their client to start adjusting himself to the idea that he would spend every day of the remainder of his life in solitary confinement, leaving his cell only for his daily period of hard labor.

After leaving Lippert to stew over his fate through the Christmas holiday, the attorneys returned with the exciting news that—due to their brilliant legal acumen and close personal relationship with Circuit Court Judge Leo W. Corkin—they had finagled the plea bargain of the century. If (and only if) they acted *immediately*, Judge Corkin would allow Lippert to plead guilty to second degree murder and entirely dismiss the first degree charge that would inevitably result in a mandatory life sentence doing hard labor. Since the sentence for second degree murder would be at the judge's discretion, there existed the possibility of leniency.

The attorneys absolutely guaranteed that the worst possible thing that could happen was that Lippert would spend ten years in prison and be a free man once again at age 27. After all, Pribble had confessed to committing the murder and described Lippert's role on the night of the crime as simply going with him to the scene of the crime and hiding behind the garage during the commission of the fatal act.

Succumbing to the pressure, Lippert appeared in Gratiot County Circuit Court in January 1971 and stood silent while his attorney explained to the court that his client was guilty of being an accomplice to second degree murder and asked to enter that plea on his client's behalf. At this point, Judge Corkin reiterated and emphasized that if Lippert did not plead guilty to the second degree murder charge, he could be found guilty of both that charge *and* the first degree murder charge. Judge Corkin then instructed Lippert to explain to the court exactly what he had done, and his attorney handed him a prepared statement to read into the record.

When the sun went down on January 26, 1971—sixteen working days after his arrest and following less than ten minutes in court—Phillip Lippert became the youngest inmate in the largest walled prison in the world at Jackson, Michigan, having been sentenced to the term of life imprisonment.

—⚋—

The appeals procedure is a vehicle by which those convicted of crimes can petition the court to review their conviction and/or sentence and remedy any errors that may have occurred during any phase of the proceedings. Anyone convicted of a felony has one Appeal of Right and is entitled to have counsel appointed by the court to assist in reviewing the record for issues that could compel some relief and in preparing that appeal to present to the court. When Lippert petitioned the court for appellate counsel in April 1971, Judge Corkin appointed one of the attorneys who had originally represented Lippert. Since the legal issues that could have led to Lippert actually having a day in court revolved around actions taken earlier by this same attorney, the attorney was faced with a ludicrous choice: he could explain to the court that the entire case against his client should be invalidated because of his own incompetence, or he could file a sworn statement with the court affirming that there had been no legal errors or judicial misconduct, that all procedures had been fair, and that his client's rights had been respected. Needless to say, he filed the affidavit without consulting his client or even reviewing the record.

Because it is such an obvious conflict of interest, the Supreme Court ruled early in the twentieth century that appointing the original defense counsel to handle an appeal is always improper. It was a violation of court rules for Judge Corkin to appoint this attorney and inappropriate for him to accept the appointment. Thus Lippert's one guaranteed right to judicial review was wasted.

Five years after his conviction, another attorney hired by Lippert's parents arranged for an evidentiary hearing to be held. This is a procedure by which evidence not previously presented is entered into the court records. Since there was almost no investigation of the crime, and a total of only seven pages of court transcripts, there were very few facts available for any reviewer. At the end of a full day of testimony by witnesses who had not been heard from previously and examination of physical evidence never before presented to the court, Judge Corkin ordered that a second hearing be held.

Included in evidence at the second hearing was a sworn statement submitted a year earlier by William Pribble which exonerated Lippert completely. The facts and circumstances set forth in this statement were thoroughly scrutinized; and a number of witnesses, as well as significant physical evidence, were examined to establish its veracity. It was reiterated beyond all doubt that Lippert played no active role in the commission of the crime and was not present when the murder took place.

At the conclusion of the second hearing, Judge Corkin issued a written opinion stating that he had doubt that Lippert was guilty at all of the crime of which he had been convicted and that obviously this was a matter that needed to be addressed by a jury trial. The original guilty plea was struck from the record and a trial date set so that all evidence could be presented to a jury, all witnesses could be examined and cross-examined under oath, and all physical evidence could be scrutinized and evaluated. Thereby, Judge Corkin wrote, the truth could be determined once and for all.

Following this pronouncement, the Gratiot County prosecutor's office went into overdrive fighting Judge Corkin's ruling. After several months of wrangling between Lippert's attorneys, Judge Corkin, and the local prosecutor, Judge Corkin reversed himself and withdrew his order for a trial. None of the newly revealed evidence had been discredited and no new evidence had surfaced. Judge Corkin exercised his right to change his mind and determined that a jury trial and examination of the evidence was not necessary after all. Lippert was returned to Jackson Prison to continue his life sentence.

At Lippert's first parole board interview in the summer of 1979, members commented on the unusual severity of his sentence. Noting that his institutional record was exemplary and that his psychological evaluations were all positive, the board declared that Lippert should be released at the conclusion of ten calendar years, the earliest any "lifer" could legally be released.

Several weeks before his release date would have been set, Lippert received a one-sentence memo from the parole board: "We have discontinued processing your release." It took months to get any explanation.

Lippert found that Circuit Court Judge Timothy Green, Judge Corkin's successor in office, had exercised a seldom-invoked technicality to veto the parole board's unanimous decision. Judge Green had also written the parole board stating emphatically that he did not want

Lippert or Lippert's family to be given any information about his involvement or the reasons for his action.

The parole board respected that request and to this day—at this printing, nearly twenty years later—have never revealed the reasons for withdrawing the parole they had previously described as "overdue," nor have they indicated what Lippert can do to gain a parole.

After informing Lippert that, instead of being released on parole, he would stay incarcerated for the remainder of his life, Jackson officials transferred him to a minimum security barracks located five miles from the main prison. After Judge Green reiterated that never, under any circumstances, would he allow Lippert to be paroled, Lippert walked out of the barracks in the spring of 1983 and set off in search of whatever life had to offer him under the circumstances.

Lippert spent most of the next five and a half years in Texas. Despite having grown to maturity in prison with no experience functioning as an adult in today's complex society, Lippert maintained steady employment, paid his bills, made friends, and in every way functioned as "normal" people do in normal circumstances. In May 1988, he was arrested near Navasota, Texas, and returned to Jackson to serve out his life sentence.

Instead of charging him with escape, a felony punishable by an extra five year sentence, prison officials considered the extenuating circumstances and declared Lippert's five and a half year absence as "institutional misconduct"—punished with three hours loss of yard privileges.

At this printing, the parole board has stated that they have no intention of releasing Lippert from prison. Ever. They have expressed "no interest" in ever interviewing him again or otherwise giving his case any further consideration.

Thus it falls to Phillip Lippert and those close to him to call attention to his unique predicament.

—〰—

Alonzo Hart's youngest daughter, Bridget, had always been disturbed by the manner in which her father's murder had been handled by Gratiot County officials. She was frustrated by the treatment she received whenever she tried to obtain any information from the local police or the

8

Gratiot County courthouse. Twenty-three years after the murder, on Father's Day in June 1993, she visited Phillip Lippert in prison. She later wrote: "What a bitter, twisted irony that I can sit in a prison visiting room with a man who pleaded guilty to involvement in my father's murder and see in him more integrity than in all of the police and court officials who represent themselves as pillars of society. In one hour with Phil I learned more than I had in many frustrating years of dealing with those in authority. Where they were always elusive and impossible to pin down to specifics, Phil was open and straightforward. What they had to say was always so convoluted and contradictory and often simply did not make any sense. What Phil told me had the ring of truth and fit the pieces of this puzzle I already had. Phil promised me early on that he would always be honest with me and he was, even when the truth was difficult or even painful for both of us."

Feeling betrayed by the system, Hart set out to raise public awareness of the situation. On July 16, 1993, Hart hand-delivered one thousand copies of an open letter door-to-door in Ithaca, detailing what she knew and suspected about her father's murder. She was immediately deluged with letters and phone calls from people expressing their unease with the events that had transpired, the secrecy, the unorthodox manner of the procedures, and the lightning speed with which Phillip Lippert had been whisked away. Many people had stories of their own to tell about dealings with various players in this drama, and many spoke only after being guaranteed anonymity. Inspired by this response, a week later Hart delivered a thousand copies of a second letter. In all, five such letters went out to the Ithaca populace.

In the ensuing months, over twelve hundred people out of a community of about three thousand wrote letters, made phone calls and signed petitions urging Michigan Governor John Engler to appoint a special investigator to examine the numerous allegations of corruption and cover-ups connected with this case. They demanded that Gratiot County court officials be held accountable for reneging on the plea bargain agreement that had been in place when Lippert was sentenced to life in prison.

Engler's only response came in the form of his legal counsel, Cheryl Arwood, telling Hart and Lippert's sister, Jennifer Weaver: "Stop sending all this junk down here. There is nothing we can do for you people."

9

Hart's efforts garnered regional and national media interest. Lippert's dilemma has been the subject of dozens of articles in various Michigan newspapers. His story was featured in a December 1993 segment of *American Journal* and was being investigated by both *A Current Affair* and *Hard Copy* when those programs were cancelled.

Early in 1994, Hart was contacted by Suzy Stein, executive director of *Donahue*. She was subsequently scheduled to appear on the first broadcast of that program's final season. Arrangements were made with Saginaw Correctional Facility for a remote unit to televise Lippert simultaneously on the same episode. Less than two weeks before the broadcast, Hart and Lippert spoke by telephone; Hart was excited about a new outfit she planned to wear for her television appearance and seemed proud of her success in being featured on *Donahue*. She believed Phil Donahue's audience of ten million viewers provided the ultimate opportunity to reveal once and for all the circumstances surrounding her father's murder and thus force the system to mete out justice to all concerned.

Shortly after that conversation, Bridget Hart, for all intents and purposes, dropped off the face of the earth. It has been determined that she is alive and well, but has relocated and is unwilling to speak with any of the people who had worked hand-in-hand with her for many months on the project. She did not accept or return calls from Suzy Stein, who was forced at short notice to substitute a different program in Hart's slot. The obvious questions related to Hart's withdrawal from her own success story have been left unanswered.

Lippert has asked from the beginning for nothing more than to be allowed his day in court. It has not been lost on observers that it is the convicted felon, the "bad guy," who has been clamoring for decades in favor of letting the system work as our forefathers intended it. He is asking only that *all* of the facts be exposed to the public, *all* witnesses examined in a public forum, and that the truth, the whole truth, and nothing but the truth finally be revealed. It is the police, prosecutors, judges, and other government officials who, in this case, have prevented justice from being done and who have circumvented and undermined the legal system.

Bridget Hart wrote in a 1993 letter: "Phil Lippert grew to adulthood in a place sociologists call 'The Monster Factory.' Miraculously, a decent human being emerged. Sometimes a man has to be standing with both feet in hot water before he is moved to put his best foot forward. That appears to be the case here. There is a difference between being tough on crime and [dispensing] mindless cruelty. That line was crossed long ago in this case. The draconian punishment inflicted upon Phillip Lippert and his family in my father's name is insulting not only to my father's legacy, but to the dignity and decency of the people of Gratiot County."

For more information, visit the website of the Phillip Lippert Defense Fund at <www.Phillip-Lippert.com>. This website was created and is maintained by Lippert's supporters; the State of Michigan does not provide computers or internet access to prisoners.

SECTION 1:
ME AND MY WIFE IRENE

WILD CARD

My wife Irene got this fancy new word processor and is taking some classes at the community college, something she's wanted to do since we got married. Now she has some homework to do and she's like a school kid again. You shoulda seen Reeny back in high school. She was a real star. People wondered how I got so lucky. Me, too. She's out right now and this is my first chance to play with this machine. It's good to be home alone—I'm still mad at her for something from last week. It was nothing, really, but it is so frustrating to be misunderstood.

Well, I guess you can tell I'm not my regular self here. Mostly, I make it a point to stay away from typewriters and other implements that can tell on me when I've had a few. I tend to get what those sensitive poet types refer to as "maudlin" (what a sissy word). I also tend to run my trap, which is very uncharacteristic for me. What happened here is, a couple weeks back I did Fat Mike a favor, not expecting nothing from it, and tonight after work, he up and lays this Party Pak on me (which is this hookup they sell that comes with tequila, triple sec, coarse salt, a couple little plastic glasses, and a shaker). Fat Mike knows—hell, everybody knows—how I feel about a margarita. What can I do? I'm a native-born Texan: it's part of my heritage. We sat there in his van and polished them babies off. I'm lit up like a Christmas tree if you really want to know.

15

When I get annoyed about Reeny not understanding something, I have to remind myself that there's a lot I don't get about her. Like her taste in movies. If I don't understand why it's important for her to go off with the girls—where she is right this minute—and pay seven hundred and fifty cents to have someone in Hollywood rip her heart out, she sure doesn't get why it means something to me to spend the same amount to go to a poker game, have a couple of beers, listen to raunchy jokes, and make a few sexist comments I don't really mean. If I don't win a single hand, I call it money well spent. Go figger.

Okay, so the poker goes a little deeper than that. It all sort of goes back to that really bad thing we went through a few years ago when I was betting on the NFL. Your average beauty queen would have up and left me and no one would have blamed her. Least of all me, but Reeny—it never entered her mind. Sometimes people are surprised that a guy like me can go around saying that my wife is so much smarter than me. (Okay, so I don't say it a lot, but people know I'm proud of my wife, okay?) She was smart enough back then to know that I could not have felt worse about it, that it wasn't humanly possible for me to be sorrier, and that I would have sold my soul to spare her and the kids all that, so she didn't find it necessary to rub my nose in it. When the whole thing reached the Critical Shit level, she hauled me out of the jug and told me we had to put our heads together and figure this thing out. It was our problem. Can you believe that? Irene Cunningham, who everyone said coulda done better, who shoulda been off somewhere being pampered and spoilt, but instead . . . well, how do you explain something like that?

What had happened was, one day I ran into this character I knew from my wild and somewhat misspent youth. Petey and me done some crazy things back in the day. About the time Irene and I got married, he moved over to New Orleans where they say he was really doing swell. When I run into him, Petey was driving a brand new El Dorado and dressed straight out of *GQ Magazine*. It's not like I envied the guy because me and Reeny was real happy. We was still kids, really—struggling to get by was kind of an adventure, and I never cared about fancy clothes and all that. Even so, I can see that Petey is onto something and I want details. Petey buys a pitcher of margaritas and goes to talking trash. Finally he tells me to put fifty bucks on the Vikings this Sunday. Fifty bucks. Right.

Why not fifty grand? Petey says trust me on this, and I just sort of held my breath, scrinched my eyes shut and forked over the grocery money. Two days later, this bookie named Sal hands me back three hundred and twenty-five American dollars. Listen, I'm just your everyday working stiff. All I ever done was sweat the rent, clip coupons and scuffle to keep the kids looking decent. Do you know how much money that is to a guy like me?

I didn't go apeshit or anything. First thing, I went grocery shopping and picked up some special treats for the kids. Next, I went out and bought this piece of jewelry I knew Reeny was in love with but didn't even fantasize about ever owning. That made me feel so good, I can't tell you. All that, and I still had enough to bet the following Sunday.

Naturally, Irene didn't like it. She didn't like Petey, never did, and she didn't like gambling, and she was scared to death of Sal. She's bending my ear about quitting while I'm ahead and blah, blah, blah. You betcha. Go over there on Eleventh Street and tell one of those crackheads to stop sucking on that glass pipe. Petey kept giving me these hot tips, and I kept winning, week after week. It was like a dream, and Reeny is steady telling me to stop! I got real nasty about it—told her to carry her ass down to the shop and put in forty hours a week on the loading dock for a few months and then tell me to turn down free money. Reeny says nothing is *true?* free. I tell her to get off my back. She didn't even know the half of it. After the second week, I was signing my paycheck over to Sal and picking up my winnings a couple days later. I borrowed money against the car and bet everything I could beg or borrow from everyone I knew. By the time the playoffs rolled around, some real money was changing hands.

Remember that really spectacular game when New England beat the Saints in double overtime and their quarterback played the whole last quarter on a busted ankle in the middle of a freaking blizzard? Well, I do. It was right after that game that my friend Petey met his untimely demise. I never got all the details. Some kind of freak accident that involved a .38 slug through the temple with his hands tied behind his back in the trunk of his car out at the airport. I don't know exactly what the scam was, but after they fished Sal out of the river sporting the same kind of headache, a couple of really well-dressed Italian guys stopped by the house to talk about some money they figured I owed them. From there it got a little crazy.

The figure that was bandied about sounded to me like the national debt. Irene went down and talked to a guy at the FBI office. Their advice: you owe these people money, it would be a good idea to pay it.

Next day, a courier service delivers an envelope to the front door. It's a picture of my kid. No note, no threat, nothing out of the way about the picture—just a snapshot of my six-year-old daughter walking to school with her little Snoopy lunch pail taken through the cross hairs of a sniper scope.

One night this fairy lawyer comes to the house and pulls a computer printout from his briefcase that outlines in detail everything we got, and what we're worth down to the last penny. They got the same info on Irene's parents. It was surreal. This guy just casually discussing all this stuff like we had invited him over and all matter-of-fact about it. He figured we can borrow this much from my in-laws (who are already crazy about me), and I can put in this much overtime at the shop, Reeny can go back to work and they'll arrange for some sleazy S&L in Baton Rouge to approve a loan for about half the money in the universe on a payment plan we can keep up and an interest rate that will buy everyone in Memphis a pink Cadillac before all's said and done. He pushes the contract over in front of me and hands me one of them thousand dollar fountain pens. I started to go off on this fag and Irene says, "Just sign it." So I did. Suddenly all those hundred dollar bills I had stuffed in that tool box in the basement were no more than peanuts.

That was a long time ago. We did everything just like they said and we never heard from them mugs again. There's a lot of things in life Reeny coulda had if we hadn't had that drain on our income for all those years, but she never said anything.

Irene keeps that cameo in a little velvet box in a drawer with this frilly, lacy stuff she used to wear before she put on that extra weight. She doesn't know that I know. She takes it out sometimes and looks at it, but she never wears it. I'm not very smart, but I know enough not to mention it.

I guess I didn't get to the part about how I get to take seven dollars and fifty cents to a penny-ante poker game every other Thursday night and all that, but Jose Cuervo has teamed up with the Sand Man and it's time to hit the sack. I want to be able to pretend I'm asleep when Reeny comes in. In spite of all we been through together, I hate for her to see me when I'm all misty.

Good night, Baby.

HOT BUTTON ISSUES

My wife Irene bailed me out of jail this morning. You can believe there is some unpleasant stuff in the air around here today. I can't believe it. I haven't been in jail since that thing with me and Petey in ninth grade. It doesn't feel very good, I can tell you that. Irene is more upset than you can imagine and quieter than I have ever known her. When Irene is not chatty, something is very wrong. Right now she is doing this thing where she is not saying anything, but it doesn't seem like "quiet" is the right word. Her silence has a screaming quality to it.

The worst of it is, I was in jail over a barroom fight. Geez, can you believe that? Maybe a dozen times in the last thirty years have I gone into a bar, and believe me, I am not a brawler. I didn't even tell you the worst of it. The other guy? He didn't go to jail. He went to the hospital. In an ambulance. All I can say is, he started it.

To understand this fiasco, you have to look back several decades. Me and Irene were living in a cozy little house in a really nice neighborhood in Austin. This was the first time either of us had lived in the city and we were loving it. This neighborhood had lots of huge old trees and a nice park and friendly neighbors. We spent a lot of time sitting on our back patio just enjoying being there.

I have to interrupt myself and tell you something about my wife Irene. To say that she was a tree-hugger doesn't quite put a fine enough point on it. Irene in those days would have been careful not to hug the tree *too hard*. You want an example? Okay. During this time, there was an alley that separated our back yard from the back yard across the way. People on both streets used it for access to their garages. I built a little privacy fence from our garage over to the neighbor's and Irene planted morning glories in front of it. Those morning glories loved that fence and pretty soon it was a solid wall of flowers. It really was pretty. Bees loved it. Right at sundown, Irene would go out and check to make sure all the little bees got home safely. Apparently, those little jokers can get exhausted and if they stay out too late, which is to say, after the sun goes down, they catch a chill and don't have the energy to fly back to the hive. They will die of exposure if they have to stay outside in the nighttime temperatures. Irene would go out there with a honey bottle and put a little drop of honey on the leaf in front of any bee that happened to be stranded there. After a few seconds, you could see its tongue flick out and slurp it up. A minute or so later, it would rev up its little engines and fly on home. Have you ever heard of such a thing? *Bees*

I told you that by way of saying if the person who spoon-feeds bumble bees laughed the night I shot my neighbor's dog, there is more to this tale than meets the eye at first glance.

Besides this idiotic situation I'm in now, I've been in two fights since high school. (The war doesn't count.) I'm from the Texas boondocks. Life out there is what you would call physical. This is a part of the world where seemingly normal people wrestle enraged eighteen hundred pound bulls for fun, where football is religion and people drink beer and fight *just because*. I'm not a kid anymore, though, and you really have to flip my switch to get me to exchanging blows with you. I have a couple different buttons that can be pushed. I'll tell you about one of them, just so you won't think I'm your everyday drunken, brawling yahoo.

Shortly after I returned from my overseas adventures, I was driving past this dive out near where I used to live and saw Fat Mike's truck in the parking lot. I hadn't seen him in a couple years and pulled in. It was good to see the old boy again. We go way back, played a lot of football together and have always been pretty tight. I can see right now you're

21

getting the wrong idea about a guy named "Fat Mike." Mike is a big boy. Even though he has always carried around a lot of padding, what you are looking at is insulation over some very solid stuff. Mike grew up on a ranch and I'll tell you something about that part of the world where we came up: They figure that if you can stand up and walk, you can toss a bale of hay. If you are out of diapers, you can bulldog a steer. Life is not soft. On top of that, Mike played football for five years in high school and one year in college before he got booted out and was drafted into the Marine Corps. He had spent three years there when I ran into him in this juke joint. He may have looked fat, but I'll tell you what, that old boy was no slob. (That was back then, you understand. Today that whole blubber-to-muscle ratio would be represented by a different set of numbers.)

Anyhow, this knucklehead Chester comes over all drunk and belligerent, trying to pick a fight with Fat Mike. Chester was a bullrider, small but wiry as hell, and a real scrapper. For all that, Fat Mike could have put him away without breaking a sweat. I'll give you a clue that tells you a lot about Fat Mike. When he played college ball, his nickname was Big Friendly. Okay? So Chester uses every insult and jibe in the book, getting himself all worked up and madder by the second. Fat Mike was just talking to him, trying to get him calmed down, and finally Chester just hauls off and smacks Fat Mike with a solid punch you could hear clear across the room, over the jukebox. Mike fires back and Chester spins around about six times before colliding with the jukebox and sort of sliding to the floor. The way Fat Mike is, he feels bad about it. He picks Chester up, dusts him off, sits him on a stool at the bar and puts a beer in front of him.

A little while later, everyone had pretty much forgotten about that little ruckus, and here comes Chester through the door with a pistol. Clear across the room, I can see that this piece is my .357. Where I come from, everyone has a pistol under the front seat of their pickup, and apparently Chester went out looking for something to work with and mine was the first open truck he came to. Then he pointed that gun at Fat Mike.

Our boy Chester had been exercising poor judgment all over the place that night and this particular act was the capper. Something inside me went ziggidy-boom and I lit into Chester in a way that, well, I may as well be honest here, when people talked about it later, the word "maniac" was used several different times. I gotta tell you, I kinda scared myself there.

So anyway, I said earlier that I have a couple buttons you can push but probably shouldn't. That's one. Don't steal my gun and point it at a friend of mine right in front of me when I've just returned from an intense and action-packed tour of duty over you-know-where. Okay?

I told you once before that Irene is pretty down to earth, for being a Liberal and all. Part of that comes from the fact that Reeny, like me, is country. In my case, we were barely more than sharecroppers, living way, way out where it was just us and the critters. Irene's family had a pretty respectable little dairy operation just outside of town. When "town" is a burg with one stoplight, though, you don't have to be very far outside of it to be officially "country." Because she grew up rubbing elbows with rattlesnakes and coyotes and saying grace over venison, wild turkey, and what have you, Irene doesn't have a problem with guns. She understands that a gun is a tool and she understands that nobody gives their potential more respect than I do. She also understands that in the world we live in, it is not unthinkable that a large-caliber equalizer can be your friend. She has never given me any grief about owning guns. During the time we lived in that little bungalow in Austin, I kept a .22 magnum in the top dresser drawer. If you think ".22" means "popgun," you don't know your weaponry. A .22 magnum with a seven-inch barrel, loaded with stinger rounds in all six chambers, will drop you and five of your closest friends in your tracks. Unless you happen to be a healthy young rhinoceros.

So where I started out was, we've been working a lot of overtime at the shop lately, on account of they are opening a branch location down in Austin. All the heavy equipment here is moving and we are getting all new stuff. Yesterday was rough. First we manhandled about a thousand tons of tools and what have you into these old Army surplus trucks—you know those kind with the canvas-covered bed?—and then rode down to Austin in the back end and unloaded them down there. That part of our twelve-hour shift we weren't busting our humps, we were packed in under canvas and, if you recall, it got up over a hundred degrees yesterday. If you think this sounds like a hot, sweaty, uncomfortable way to bring home the bacon, you can congratulate yourself for being what they call a very perceptive person.

23

Once we got everything unloaded and called it a day, the guys were talking about stopping at Roxie's for a pitcher of cold brewski before heading back home. Hey, I'll tell you what—that sounded like a damned awful good idea at that point in my life. Are you kidding? I mean, it was *hot* out there yesterday. When's the last time I was in a place like Roxie's? Or any kind of bar, for that matter. I honestly can't remember, but it was rare enough that the guys were having a lot of fun with it—shouldn't you call Irene and get permission? Is your missus going to be mad at us for bringing you here? That kinda stuff. I'm the guy at work who always goes straight home after. I know it's weird, but I like to hang out with my wife. I'm with the guys all day at work. I'll let you in on a little secret— I've had enough of those clowns by lunchtime.

I know I said before I've had a couple of fights since high school. Since you may be wondering about the other one, I'll go ahead and tell you that story too. I may as well talk to you because I'm not getting a lot of conversation back at the castle right now.

This was a crappy situation right from the word "go." I'm mad at myself more than anything for even getting into the car with Elmo. Right away, you gotta figure a guy named Elmo is going to be bad news. I've known this dork for years and I never liked him. Blame it on my roots. I don't like a white guy who finds it necessary to talk jive like a ghetto gang-banger, especially if he is from Small Town, Texas. The series of circumstances that all accidentally came together to make me hook up with Elmo and let him carry me off into the night are so twisted and complicated that, oh geez, I don't want to go through all that. Let's just say I was goofy enough to say, "Okay, Elmo, let's go," and start the story at that point. So now we're on the road headed to San Antonio to see this guy Herbie that Elmo knows from God knows where and that I need to get in touch with. There and back by ten o'clock. We get to San Antonio and, naturally, this clown we're looking for is nowhere to be found. Certainly not where Elmo knew for a certainty he would be. So then we had to make the rounds. We bop in and out of half a dozen topless bars, each time me dragging Elmo back out once it's determined that old boy isn't there. Some of these places have a cover charge and I gotta pay it because if I don't go in with him, this hockey puck will forget about me after the first bump and grind. A couple hours of this and I want to grab Elmo by his scrawny hip-hop neck.

Right about the time Elmo's neck was on the verge, you understand, we run into Herbie's brother-in-law, who gives us an address in Houston and says, yeah, zip on down, he'll be happy to see you. At this point, we were on the deep south side of San Antonio, closer to Houston than to Austin anyway, and I felt like I had a major investment in this project already and screw it, let's bop down to Houston.

The address we found in Houston was in the Fifth Ward. In case you are not familiar with the crappier side of Houston, Texas, Fifth Ward is an area where people put their kids to bed in the bathtub because, chances are, any stray bullets won't penetrate it. No kidding: as bad neighborhoods go, Fifth Ward makes South Bronx look like Hollywood Hills by comparison. The address we had was Herbie's in-laws. They lived in this really tiny one bedroom apartment. There was this postage stamp of a living room, with a microscopic bedroom off to one side and a kitchenette on the other. They had a bathroom like you find in a camper van or something. The thing of it is, these were really decent people. They were a couple probably in their early fifties, just down-home, hard-working Christian people. They tell us we just missed this guy, but say we can find him downtown at a joint called Echoes. I have heard of Echoes. Hey, I ain't going down there. Period. Blow it off, man, carry me back up to Austin. Elmo tells me, "Oh no, baby boy, chill, we be all right. They *know* me down there." Elmo talks plenty of trash, but nothing is getting me to carry my pale face into Echoes. He asks these folks is it all right for me to stay there for ten minutes while he zips down and grabs Herbie and jets right back. There and back, ten minutes, tops. With a notable lack of enthusiasm, they say okay. Ten minutes, right?

At the end of one hour, I'm pretty sure Elmo will lose teeth when I see him again. At the end of two hours, the situation is excruciating. These people don't have a television or anything, so there is just a whole lot of very uncomfortable sitting around watching the clock. By this time, it's late at night, and these are people who have to get up and go to work in a few hours. Probably jobs that demand physical exertion and probably by way of public transportation, and hey, they need their sleep.

25

At the same time, like I said, these are decent people. They aren't going to just put me out. This is the Fifth Ward. You don't just toss a lone white boy out there in the wee hours. I had like seven bucks in my pocket, and even if I had some money, taxi cabs don't come down here after dark. I'm a couple miles from the bus station, and where am I going to go on seven bucks? Out of the parking lot?

Finally the guy walked down to a pay phone on the corner and called up this minister who came over and, in the end, decided he really couldn't offer much. It was too late to get me into a shelter for the night. I asked him to just take me to the Grey Dog. By the time we left, I had spent three and a half hours with those people and I have never felt like such a lump. I exhausted my entire vocabulary trying to make them understand how sorry I was for imposing on them like that and how grateful I was to them for being so good about it. Make a long list of negative emotions, and every one of them was raging in me at that moment.

The Grey Dog in Houston is on the far north end of town. I had gone there just for some place to be, but for some reason remembered that this guy I barely knew in high school lived on the southern outskirts of San Antonio. His number was actually in the book, so I gave him a call and said I would give him a hundred bucks to come down, pick me up and get me home, but he couldn't get paid until we got to Austin. Strangely enough, about an hour and a half later, he actually showed up.

On the ride back, I end up telling him about my evening and he says, "Elmo? You don't mean jiveass wish-he-was-black Elmo?" As a matter of fact, yeah, I tell him. Talk about your coincidences, he says. When I called, he was just coming through the door. He'd been down at the Doll House, which is one of those joints Elmo dragged me into earlier. Elmo was there when he left, he tells me. You know what? I don't even care what happened. I have no interest or curiosity regarding the story of what transpired in Elmo's life from the time he left me in Fifth Ward and when he ended up back at the Doll House. I can tell you this, though, nothing else in my life mattered except that I come face to face with that fool.

I can honestly tell you I didn't have anything on my mind when I went through the door of the Doll House. I was on automatic pilot. What I remember mostly is the look on Elmo's face for that brief moment from when he looked up and saw me and when I was all over him like a well-oiled machine. It was not a pretty thing.

I more or less came to my senses when a couple of Mexican guys I didn't know sort of peeled me off of this idiot. I was aware of several things at once. There was a swathe of overturned furniture, broken glassware, and some very upset lap dancers across the room. And a couple of Bexar County's finest were coming through the door. These guys hustled me out a fire exit and, after a quick conversation in Spanish, told me to jump into their low rider. They carried me all the way to my front door and wouldn't even let me pay them for their trouble. *Muchos gracias, hermanos.*

Anyway, that's another button I have. That thing Elmo did? Don't ever do that to me, okay?

So anyway, all that is the background you need to understand this situation I am currently in. Except for one more thing. Directly across the alley from where our garage was in Austin, there was the garage of this old boy named Leo, who was the neighborhood fix-it man. He was a funny old geezer, a retired guy who spent a lot of time at everyone's kitchen table in the neighborhood, fixing everything from toasters to diesel engines, gossiping over coffee and dessert. He had a little workshop in his back yard and was always making toys and go-carts and what have you for kids on the block. Next door to him was a clod named Les.

This is where the trouble all began. Les brought home a Labrador mutt one day and staked it to a post in his back yard. And left it. This poor animal was anchored to a very short leash with no cover. What was Les thinking? Soon this dog goes to barking and doesn't stop. I'm telling you, the dog does not pause for a breath. Around the clock it is "arp arp arp arp arp arp arp." He is telling the world he is miserable and begging for relief.

In Texas, there is an unwritten law about messing with a man's dog that rates right up there with cattle rustling. Even so, hey, I needed some shut-eye. We didn't have air conditioning or anything and slept with the windows open, and this poor mutt was taking a toll on me. I had a job then doing hot tar roofing, and even a strapping young buck like myself needed plenty of rest to tackle that on a daily basis.

I don't know, it was maybe the fourth night of this non-stop arping, about two-thirty or so, I threw the sheet back and grabbed that magnum pistol. Dressed in boxer shorts and Irene's little plastic flip-flop sandals, I walked up on that miserable mutt and planted a stinger right between his baby blues. You have to understand about this pistol. The sound of it is like a gigantic "Pop!" Loud as a shotgun. In the middle of the night, between two houses, that was the loudest noise I'd ever heard in my life. It sort of jarred me back to reality, and I broke and ran back up the alley, through my garage, across the back yard and sort of dove into bed.

Here's the wild part. Irene was laying there laughing like the funniest thing in life had just happened. I mean, she couldn't even catch her breath. It suddenly hit me what was so funny about it. It was the sound effects. Try to imagine. First we have, for days on end, mind you, arp, arp, arp, arp, arp, arp, arp—POP!—silence. Then this frantically paced flip-flop, flip-flop, flip-flop, flip-flop, flip-flop with me running up the alley. It really was hysterical.

A couple days later, Leo stops by and tells me that he was just having coffee with Mrs. Childers down the street and the first thing she said was that she was sure glad I'd finally had enough of that damn dog. "And I want to tell you, I appreciate it, too. In fact, everyone in the neighborhood appreciates that," Leo says.

"How is it that everyone assumes it was me?" I asked as innocently as I could. Leo told me to look around at all the houses where people could have heard that dog. "Now which of those people are going to come out in the middle of the night and shoot someone's dog?" He had me there. By process of elimination, it was me.

Now I had a new concern. "What do you think, Leo? Am I going to have trouble with Les about this?"

"I don't rightly think so," Leo says. "Hell, only thing that old boy knows about you is that you got a gun."

This might be hard to believe, I don't know, but for all intents and purposes, me and Irene been married since junior high. By the time we graduated, I had forgotten there were other women on the planet. At this stage of my life, I'm pretty sure there aren't. We're sitting at this table in Roxie's and all I see is a sweaty pitcher of ice cold draft floating across the room in my direction. This is going to be good going down. It didn't even register that the pitcher was being conveyed across the room by a nubile young cupcake who had forgotten to put on a shirt. I work outdoors. It got up over a hundred degrees yesterday. Twelve hour shift. Just a glass or two, that's all I want.

Suddenly, out of nowhere, some caveman is in my face telling me all kinds of nasty things about myself, describing some very unpleasant things he intends to inflict upon my person. *What the hell?* My response is to try to reason with him—hey, you got the wrong guy, what are you talking about? Here, have a beer, let's talk about this. Not such a big man without your guns, are you? he asks me. I'm still confused. What *is* this? Finally, after a whole lot of drunken sputtering and carrying on, I realize this doorknob is my old neighbor, Les. This is about me shooting his mutt. What was that, thirty years ago? I can't believe it. Les wants to fight. I offer him a beer for the second time, and he slaps the pitcher off the table. That was his first mistake.

At this point in my life, I really got nothing to prove. There was a time I couldn't live with myself if I let someone talk to me like that. Today, you want to think I'm some kind of a sissy or something—hey, I can't find the words to tell you how much I don't care. All I could think of was, how do I make this bozo go away so we can get another pitcher over here.

It finally got to the point where Les was winding down—we're not talking about someone here with an unlimited vocabulary or a whole lot of imagination—and I'm thinking this is almost over with. One thing that separates a certifiable idiot from your everyday clodhopper, though, is knowing when to quit. Les was certifiable. He could have just hitched up his britches and strolled off like the toughest dog in the junkyard. He would have had a story to tell to all his idiot friends. Instead, he got himself to believing there was nothing whatsoever he could say that would make me fight. He just had to take that one extra step and throw out a couple of comments about Irene.

First of all, during the time Les had known her, Irene could have stepped out of one of those magazines. I'm proud to tell you, she ain't no slouch now, but back then—hey, Reeny turned heads. In the past few years, she has picked up a dress size or two, which doesn't bother me, but I have a serious problem with some whiskey-soaked box of rocks in a topless bar making reference to my better half's physical self in any manner whatsoever. The particular references Les made aren't something I'm going to repeat, but I will tell you that he found it necessary to make comparisons to some of your less wholesome barnyard animals.

Irene? *My* Irene? The rescuer of tuckered-out honeybees and stray cats? The nice lady who massages my feet and fixes my favorite meals even when it's a lot of hassle and she really doesn't feel like it? Oh no, no, no, Les. You don't understand.

Okay, maybe I didn't say that. I don't think I actually said much of anything at that point, but I'm pretty sure I managed to bring home to Les the gravity of his error. There is such a thing as the One Too Many rule, and Les broke it.

That whole thing Les had to say—that pretty much represents another button I have that you can push but probably shouldn't, okay?

The hell of it is, I never did get that glass of beer.

TRUCK STOP

My wife Irene went with me last week to deliver a load of scrap metal to an out-of-state dealer. I pick up a few extra bucks pushing this rig for a friend of mine when one of his drivers is down. Reeny gets a kick out of it so I like to take her along. If things had been a little different, this here is what I'd be doing for a living, but I got that black mark on my driving record that won't go away. A thing like that, you just can't explain it, and even if you could, on paper it says I was responsible for an accident that resulted in a fatality. That's serious business.

At a truck stop somewhere outside Peoria, Irene picked up one of those newspapers with all the Elvis sightings and alien babies. There is this story about these two elderly widow sisters who are raising a couple dozen children on some hard-scrabble farm in Alabama. These people are so poor they trap sparrows for food but won't accept any handouts. So Reeny reads this story and right away gets all weepy on me (which means she thinks it's a beautiful thing—go figger). She says these people are *so strong*. The way Reeny is, she hears about a hungry person in the next county and she's reaching for her car keys. I could tell you stories about characters she has drug home and sat down at our dinner table. I haven't always been all that nice about it, if you want to know the truth of it. I mean, *come on*, you know?

31

I usta drive a truck years ago, before we got married. I worked on a big ranch out in the Hill Country and eventually worked my way into that plum position of being the guy who delivered livestock to auctions, slaughterhouses, and what have you. Before that, I was a cowboy. Think that's kinda neat? Think again. Don't even get me started. Suffice it to say that romantic picture of the Texas cowboy is pure myth. Put me in the cab of a Peterbilt any day.

That's what I was driving the day I had that bad accident just outside of San Antonio, hauling a load of Nubian dairy goats. I ran off the road, the tandem trailers jack-knifed, the hitch snapped, and the whole magilla flipped over into the Guadeloupe River, drowning every last one of them little beggars. And that was the least of it. I had to go to the hospital, went through a legal nightmare you wouldn't believe, and lost my OTR license. After that, nobody would even talk to me. When you can't get work cowboyin'—believe me, you've hit rock bottom.

Which brings me to another point I made that really irritated Irene. I know about being poor. I can relate to that business of having some change and counting it over and over, like maybe it went forth and multiplied in your pocket. That's why I think they should make it a law that poor people all live out in the country. They may not ever have much, but at least they wouldn't have to be hungry. I'm speaking from experience here. It don't cost much of nothing at all to keep yard birds, the rivers are full of fish, and pretty much any critter you can pull out of the woods will make a meal. That's not to mention keeping a garden. And these people are eating sparrows? I've eaten pigeon before, and I can tell you there is not much of a meal there. Sparrows? I don't get it.

Like I said, those kind of observations just drive Reeny up the wall. She gets so exasperated trying to make me see *the point*. This is where she tells me I think just like a man (which I gather is not a good thing) and pretty much gives up.

So last week, I took Irene along on a run from Detroit to San Diego. She somehow got onto the subject of why we would all be better off with a woman president. In case you haven't guessed, my better half is a Liberal. Without really giving it much thought, I expressed a somewhat different perspective and ended up saying quite a lot more than I had intended to. Just on the far side of Joplin, Missouri, it strikes me that the old girl is real quiet and has been for a while. Never a good sign. I knew this was going to be a long, uncomfortable trip if I didn't do something radical, and do it quick. That's how she finally got the whole story out of me about that accident out there on Loop 410 that day. She'd been working on me for years and I would never give up a peep. Now I just came clean and spilled it. I gotta say, she was good about it. She just said, "I didn't know you liked V-8 juice." It was a good sixty-five miles down the road before she cracked up. It started with this sort of muffled sound like when you try to hold in a sneeze, and built all the way up to side-splitting, teary-eyed laughter like a cartoon character getting the old feather-tickle treatment. I didn't get upset about that. I figure an hour is about the statute of limitations on a story like that. Reeny said that if anyone else in the world had told her that story, nothing could've made her believe it. Me, things like that just seem to come my way. Don't ask me why.

What I tried to make Irene understand about these people eating sparrows is that there is something actually selfish about refusing to let anyone give you a helping hand when you need it. Especially when they're in the business themselves of helping all these kids they're raising. There is a certain brand of Christianity that embraces the idea that if you aren't miserable, you aren't righteous. Kinda guy I am, I gotta wonder, what's so great about being hungry and uncomfortable? I personally have been there, and I'll tell you quite honestly, it didn't strike me as a particularly spiritual experience.

So anyway, on those small cans of V-8 juice like they sell in little country stores—you know how they have this little rectangle of aluminum foil stuff over the hole? I usta take a bunch of these babies along to sip on while I was driving, okay? But what would happen is, when I zipped that little tab off the top, it would sort of say "blip" and a squirt of it would jump out and land right where I didn't want it to. I was always sweating and grubby and not fit for lickin', so I would have this stuff dripping off my hand, getting all sticky and yucky. I had all this paperwork I needed to keep neat and it would end up with splotches of goop all over it. Trust me, it was a mess. I used to obsess on weird stuff; a normal person would've just gotten the next larger size can with the pull-tab top. I took it personally—it was me or the V-8 can.

So what happened was, I was holding the steering wheel with my knees and used both hands to hold the little can up to my mouth. My thinking was that I would zip that little sucker open and catch the squirt on my tongue. I win. If you've ever opened one of those jokers, you've heard it release that vacuum of air that gets trapped inside. Let me tell you something: there is some real power in that little can. What happened was, as soon as I peeled that aluminum strip back, that little *phhht* sound sort of sucked the tip of my tongue into the hole in the top of the can. And I mean *for real*. Now I'm gear-jamming a Peterbilt long-nose tractor with a double trailer rig full of very agitated dairy goats at sixty-five miles per hour in heavy traffic with a tin can hanging onto the tip of my tongue. I couldn't get that sucker loose. It wouldn't let go. When I tried to twist it off, it cut into my tongue on both sides. You want a whole new perspective on Something That Really Stings? Slice open your tongue and pour some V-8 juice into the cut. I was trying to keep my head, but really, how do you act in this type of situation? I went to truck driver school and everything and believe me, they never covered this particular contingency. I'm driving with both hands now, but my eyes are tearing up and pretty soon, hey, I can't even see. Naturally I'm in a center lane, and by the time I can get over and catch an exit, I'm pretty much driving blind.

It would've been bad enough if this had been your everyday big deal parade. What they had going on was some kind of Chamber of Commerce thing emphasizing businesses in the area and all that. There was a ten-foot-tall Tootsie Roll, there was a guy in a Pillsbury Dough Boy costume, there was the Jolly Green Giant on stilts towering over everyone. I think I saw the Michelin Man, too. I didn't actually see Mr. Peanut, but I sure heard about him. And what's a parade without elephants? Where is that written, anyway? Must be the guy who rents out all those parade elephants got it written into law somewhere that you cannot have a dumbass parade anywhere in America without elephants. Ever notice how big them suckers are? Big as a dinosaur, fresh out of the jungle, and people are surprised that one of them freaks out when a semi tractor with both stacks blowing coal-black smoke and all twenty wheels bouncing comes screaming off cross-country straight at him.

If Dumbo had squashed the Holly Farms lady or bowled over the Wendy's Hamburger girl, I'd still be in Huntsville. Lawyer said it helped me a lot when the judge chuckled at the prosecutor describing the scene of a four-ton Asian elephant running off cross country holding a six-foot peanut over his head like he'd just made the heist of the century. Apparently, the elephant didn't notice that the peanut had arms and legs. The coroner said that the old boy actually died of a heart attack and that he had a long history of related health problems. That helps but, geez, who wants to be a part of something like that? People also chuckled when the guy got up there to explain how they had to surgically remove a vegetable juice can from my tongue. I was grateful for the stitches, though; I had a good excuse for not saying much.

I don't know how we got from those poor people eating sparrows and refusing charity all the way over to my more embarrassing personal problems. That seems to happen a lot lately. I think I'm going to shut up for about a week.

MOTHER HUBBARD

My wife Irene, the author, is all excited. Some little magazine printed a story she wrote, which is based on an event from my childhood. She never heard the whole story, which she would have loved, but Reeny, she's funny in some ways, and I know what to leave out of my stories. Me and the missus, we been together so long, we look alike. We don't even have to speak anymore; I know when her feet ache, she knows when I'm peeved at some slob down at the shop. That's why I have to be careful. If I even touched on these other topics, she would know immediately that she was not the very first woman I was ever in love with. Neither of us needs that. It wouldn't even matter that it was years before Irene and I met in junior high.

I never went through that "I Hate Girls" stage. Ruthie Zimmerman and I found each other in third grade. Ruthie was so smart, she just killed me. If she didn't know something, she knew how to figure it out. One time she took me to this place in the courthouse where you could just walk right in and get information and stuff on just about any topic in the world. She got some pamphlets on breast-feeding babies and some other terrifying stuff I didn't even want to think about. I got some info on catching varmints in live traps.

Sad to say, I peaked in third grade and crashed and burned in fifth. The neatest thing about third grade was that we were both in Mrs.

Hubbard's room. Mrs. Hubbard was already a little old lady then; she wasn't much bigger than your average third grader and always wore these enormous hats and carried purses you could use for smuggling elephants. She delighted in calling herself Mother Hubbard. At the thirtieth anniversary of our graduating class, people were saying "Remember Mother Hubbard?" How many third grade teachers have that kind of legacy?

Anyway, Ruthie was, and continued on to be, the smartest girl there ever was in our school. She thought I was cute and loved my dinosaur-erasers-in-the-nostrils schtick (you had to be there). She was also impressed with the idea that I had a paper route and was what she termed "an independent entrepreneur." I was on top of the world back then; there was a lot of little dudes wanted to be in my P.F. Flyers. A couple years later, the eraser thing had played out, the commies launched Sputnik, and Ruthie sent me a note, through her personal courier, Big Butt Bonnie Billings, telling me all kinds of unpleasant things about myself, including, but not limited to, the fact that I was in training to become a professional ditch digger.

What everybody remembers about Mother Hubbard was her story "The Old Lady Who Lived In The Vinegar Bottle." This was a truly wonderful tale that was delivered—not just told, recited, or read, but delivered with such gusto and enthusiasm, we were all totally enthralled. It was always a treat to get "The Story." This wasn't something to just sit through. First thing was to push all the desks to the back of the room and sit in a semi-circle on the floor. Ruthie and I held hands while Mother Hubbard delivered a one-woman show any Broadway prima donna would have been proud to claim. Then, after school, Ruthie would help me fold papers and make the rounds with me. We would usually stop off and get a strawberry shake or something after, seeing as how I was a working man and always had some change in my pocket. Life was good.

When Sputnik went up, the American educational system went into spasms. There was serious alarm over the idea that the Reds were winning the space race. I couldn't understand how a baseball team was pulling this off or why it was cause for excitement. It was out of this panic, though, that greater minds than mine decided The Answer lay in teaching New Math. That's why I blame the commies for my downfall.

Anyway, the part I started out to tell you was, one night after I got home from my paper route, I dumped out my collection money to count it and the weirdest thing happened. One of my nickels broke in half. Closer inspection revealed that it had actually been machined to come apart and that it was hollow inside. I thought someone had given me something out of a Cracker Jacks box and showed it to my dad. He was not amused. You could tell he recognized this nickel as something nefarious. He took some real fine tweezers and pulled a little bitty strip of plastic out of the slot in the nickel and held it up to the light. And freaked. Which is to say, this muscle in his cheek kinda twitched and his eyes sort of squinted in a certain kind of way. (That's about the most you are gonna get out of my pop by way of an excited reaction. Believe me, that was a big one.) He put it in a little envelope and took it downtown to the Federal Building. After that, things got goofy.

"Goofy" was pretty much the theme for life in general at this time. It became immediately apparent that some kids, who had been perfectly comfortable with everyday arithmetic, were utterly lost with this new, improved stuff that was dividing fifth grade into three groups: The Smart Class, The So-Sos and The Damn Dummies. There was no shame in being a So-So; everyone knew that New Math was hard. Being in the Smart Class was a social status to be envied. The Damn Dummies were shunned. Every morning at ten, everyone would get up and go to their respective rooms for math class. This was a big thrill also because we were changing classes, just like they do in high school. Naturally, Ruthie and I sat right next to each other in the Smart Class. By this time, we were really a serious item, and she was going with me almost every night to deliver papers.

I have come to realize over the years that that little strip of plastic was a piece of microfilm. A couple of those guys in wing tip shoes and Robert Hall suits came to the house and interrogated me endlessly about it. They went over a list of my customers and asked me thousands of questions about each of them. They asked me all kinds of questions about every store I went into and might have made change in, and all kinds of junk. Then they grilled my parents and sisters about their activities. They wanted to know what magazines we subscribed to and if we went to church regularly. It got real stupid. My dad was adamant about us having to be cooperative, this was (rather breathlessly) "The FBI," and it was important they do their job, and we don't know what all is involved in this, and all that slightly awed stuff. We were all sworn to silence.

The part I never told anybody was that it was Ruthie's nickel. I know because I only had one nickel in my bag that night, and Ruthie had put in two dimes and a nickel and took out a quarter when we stopped for Cokes earlier. She never had any idea what a ruckus her nickel created.

Like any good performer, I knew when a routine was past its prime. I got rid of the dinosaurs and moved on to more creative endeavors. I wasn't paying attention to the signs, though. Ruthie had told me more than once to "grow up" and stop goofing off in class all the time. She was impressed with the little creatures I made out of clay and bits and pieces of things laying around, but she adopted this very adult position about "a time and place for everything." I was quite confident she would come around. There is no describing the look on her face the day Mrs. Horrible (remember fifth grade?) announced that I would no longer be a part of the Smart Class, but had been demoted to the So-So group. The room was still; I was in shock, Ruthie's expression reflected a combination of betrayed horror, humiliation, and disgust. That night I delivered my papers alone.

When I went home, there was a van parked in the driveway of the house across the street. The sign on the side read Jiffy Vacuum Cleaner Repair. It had a little upright vacuum cleaner on top, and if you watched closely, you could see the handle swivel left and right occasionally. After about a week, we all started to wonder what on earth could be wrong with an 88-year-old man's vacuum cleaner that the repair people were putting in so much time over there.

My second day in the Not-Real-Stupid But-Not-Too-Swift class, I was busy constructing the prototype of a helicopter that would defeat anything the Soviets could put in the air and would, I had no doubt, save the Free World from the Crimson Tide, when I was rudely interrupted by the teacher. You know that little strip of metal that runs along the top of a wooden ruler to give you a nice, reliable straight edge? Well, I had just peeled mine off and inserted it down into an ink pen cartridge to form my rotor assembly when she attacked. The only warning I had was this figure rushing toward me saying something about this big "affair" I was having with my "toys."

On the word "affair" she snatched my rotor and on "toys" slam-dunked it into the wastepaper basket. What she didn't realize right away was that, as any physics major can tell you, two things cannot occupy the same space at the same time. You slide a little strip of metal into a ink pen and the ink has to go somewhere else. It was just as this phenomenon of nature was expressing itself—which is to say, the ink was squishing out—that the whole magilla was snatched away from me. By the time the Math Nazi realized the gravity of her error, she had ink on both hands and all over her dress. All of a sudden, she was standing over me screeching like a banshee and generally being very threatening and intimidating. I made some type of really astute observation like, "I didn't ask you to grab my helicopter," which did not serve to calm her down at all. When she drew back like Mighty Casey At The Bat, I knew enough to duck.

Under different circumstances, it may well have been amusing to recount the spectacle of this old girl swinging with all her steam, hitting thin air, and corkscrewing around three or four times. As it was, she had this glob of ink on her fingers, which sort of flung off and hit Barbara Ann Rogers right in one of her baby blues. Now we've got two screaming ban-shees, and the Math Nazi is diving over the desk to grab a handful of me by the hair. That look in her eye tells me it's time to—as we all felt so clever saying in those days—make like a bakery truck and haul my buns outta there. Which I did.

As I mentioned earlier, I came out of one of those traditional American homes where authority is never wrong. They didn't want to hear about my offended rotor assembly or the maniacal glint in the Nazi's eye. I'll spare you the details, but say it like this: if that happened today, I know a couple of parents who would be facing serious child abuse charges.

Next day, soon as I got to school, I was informed that for the remain-der of the year, I would take math with the Damn Dummies. I was mor-tified. Immediately after lunch, I received that fateful delivery from Big Butt Bonnie, and when I got home after school, I was informed that the paper I worked for would no longer be requiring my services. Apparently, several of my customers called to complain about me sending the FBI to harass them or some such thing. Ruthie called to ask about taking over the route, and they told her there was no such thing as a girl paperboy.

When my dad got home and heard about that, he was pissed. Authority is to be revered, but a man's job is sacred. He went over and banged on the side of the van until one of those clowns came out. He told them that "this ends right here. We don't see you guys again, we don't hear from you again, or have any indication of you putzing around in our lives," or else he is going to contact every news outlet he can find and tell how the FBI is accusing a snot-nose kid of being a foreign agent. It was a rather lengthy diatribe. After it was over, they sat there for about twenty minutes and then left. For good. The end.

That was also the end of my career as class clown. After that, I was real still and used the spare time to nurture my Bad Attitude. I have learned no math from that day to this. In junior high, I caught the attention of a really cute cheerleader who was also an honor student, raising once again the age-old conundrum "Why Do Good Girls Like Bad Boys?" I would see Ruth sometimes (the "ie" was dropped in sixth grade), and we'd speak, but by this time, we were on widely divergent paths.

Last summer was Mother Hubbard's one hundredth birthday. I sent her a card and wrote a few lines and got a very sweet little note back from her almost immediately. She remembered me. I was really kinda choked up. So I don't even have to tell you that Reeny was a wreck. She must have gone though four boxes of Kleenex over that. Geez. I heard later that one day last summer Ruth Zimmerman was in town (she's a big-shot lawyer now, off in The Big City), and that she went to visit Mrs. Hubbard while she was here. She asked for one last recitation of "The Old Lady Who Lived In The Vinegar Bottle" and was told okay, but only if Ruth would push the furniture back and sit on the floor and listen to the story as it was meant to be listened to. Which she did. When I heard that, I said, "God bless you, Ruthie Zimmerman." Then I thought—what I wouldn't give to have sat there with her and held her little hand during that encore performance.

Mother Hubbard died recently. What is sad is that this was in the days before everyone owned a video camera. That old lady in the vinegar bottle is lost forever now, and that is a shame.

Anyway, when Reeny wrote her story, she didn't know the part about Ruthie, or Mother Hubbard, or the Math Nazi. It might have made it a better story, and might help her understand why I still can't do long division. But Ruthie Zimmerman is one of those memories I am very stingy with, and if I mention her name around Irene, she will be the topic of conversation around our house for the next six months. I'll have to relive all of the above over and over again. Who needs that?

REGULAR ERNIE

Me and my wife Irene took a drive upstate to visit my friend Regular Ernie who is in, as we so politely say these days, "rehab." Okay, first of all, I don't want to hear any cracks about that. The man has had a rough time and he deserves better than a bunch of weisenheimers making tacky observations out the side of their faces.

The uncomfortable thing about the trip is that me and the missus are not on what you would call real friendly terms right now. This was not exactly a chatty Sunday drive in the country. I don't really care to discuss all that, though, so if you would be good enough to give me a little personal space here, I'll thank you. I'll tell you this much, though: it's not like this is about something that I did to her—like anyone is going to believe that.

There's a handful of us been friends since we was kids. We all had big plans, but after every last one of us was drafted and went through that whole thing, this little burg is where we all sunk our roots. Out of our little group, we got us three Ernies. We got Black Ernie, who is, well, black. Then we got Slick Ernie, who lost all his hair after being struck by lightning. I mean *all* his hair. No eyelashes, none of those annoying little nose hairs, zip. You see him wet and the word "slick" immediately comes to mind. Kinda creeps me out, if you want to know the truth of it. Then we

43

got Regular Ernie, who is just your everyday Joe. The thing about Regular Ernie is, he's the smartest man I ever knew. No kidding. The man is a thinker. Being a bit quirky, though, there's no such thing as higher education or regular employment or anything like that for him. For the past couple years, Regular Ernie has been a chimney sweep. In the years before that, he found what he refers to as gainful employment in such areas as underwater welding, water tower painting, skyscraper window washing, and—no kidding—gator wrestling with some dog and pony show in the Australian outback. He says that after he gets out of rehab, he might go to work on his father-in-law's used car lot. We'll see.

I guess Regular Ernie is what you would call my best friend. I have known him all my life and we have been through some significant stuff together. I stayed there with him after we broke through the floor and into the root cellar of an old barn we were exploring and Regular Ernie broke his leg and got snakebit all at the same time. We were both pretty sure he was going to die right there, and truth to tell, he was just about knocking on heaven's door by the time the calvary arrived. We talked about some pretty serious stuff during that hour or so and, believe me, guys like me and Regular Ernie don't sit around having conversations like that every day. Even as kids. I'll spare you a bunch of examples that wouldn't mean that much to you, but we have a lifetime of "firsts" and other wild experiences that we went through together. I'm just saying, a bond forms after a few decades of that kind of stuff. We don't get all sloppy about it or anything, but even Gladys and Irene know that Regular Ernie and I communicate on a level they can't touch. Drives 'em crazy.

Anyway, the major thing going on here is Regular Ernie. I'll tell you something that's none of your business because I don't want you walking around thinking that this man is just your everyday lush or something. During the war, Regular Ernie was a tunnel rat. Do you know what those guys did? Over there where we were, there were zillions of tunnels everywhere. Whenever we came up on one, someone had to squiggle down through there and take a look-see. There might be important stuff or even enemy troops down there, so you couldn't ignore it, and it might be a ton of high explosive, so you couldn't just toss a grenade down there and call it good. Some of those tunnels went on for miles, with chambers dug out here and there along the way. This was one of those jobs they almost never ordered someone to do. It was just too hairy. The wild thing is that there was always some guy who would volunteer. Some guys did their whole tour with that as their specialty. Why? You really gotta wonder, don't you? Chances are that someone is down there waiting to slice your face off with a macheté as soon as you pop your head in. The life expectancy of a tunnel rat was something like two seconds. Those guys went through hell on a good day, and there were a lot of bad days.

Try to imagine what it would be like to go wriggling down through one of those long, dark tunnels. They were built and used by munchkin-sized people, so your average full-grown G.I. had a tight go of it. It was not unheard of for a guy to just get stuck thirty or forty feet in. And then what? A lot of these tunnels were booby-trapped. What kind of nightmare would it be to get wedged in at the curve of a pitch-black underground passageway, holding a flashlight in your teeth, and realize that you just tripped the release on a cage of poisonous snakes or scorpions, and here they come. Sometimes a tunnel rat would come into one of those chambers and find the remains of some POWs who had been tortured to death and left there just for the effect it would have on whoever found them. All kinds of stuff—I don't want to get too graphic. Let's just say it was a stressful lifestyle and Regular Ernie was not the only one of those guys who came home a little quirky. People who study these things say that you come back from war with some grooves in your brain that you didn't have going in. I can believe that. Regular Ernie is a smart guy, but I'm sure he has no explanation for why he did two complete tours of duty in that particular line of work.

Anyway, Irene has been taking these classes at the community college and is currently learning everything there is to know about the American short story. You can tell she's becoming an expert because of the way she puts so many syllables into the word lit-ter-a-chew-er these days. She likes to read these stories to me and then point out the deep, hidden meanings. Some of the stories are pretty interesting and Irene is a good reader, so mostly I don't mind, but I get a little impatient with all the in-depth analysis. I mean, why not just *say it?* What is it with all this hiding little clues in the story so that people have to figure out what is really going on behind the scenes?

Let me tell you something about my better half. Mostly Irene is pretty down-to-earth and no more of a knucklehead than anybody else's wife. It's the damnedest thing about Reeny when it comes to movies, though. If a movie doesn't tear her heart out by the roots and reduce her to a sobbing mass of jelly right there on the spot, she feels cheated. Being an insensitive macho slob, I go to the movies for entertainment. Is there not enough grief and yuck in the world that I need to fork over a perfectly good portrait of Honest Abe so I can cry my eyes out over Debra Winger having cancer and Jack Nicholson being a typical man about it? I tell her—your idea of a good time is to spend the evening bawlin' and squallin', give me the five bucks and I'll kill your cat.

For the record, my idea of a good movie is *Die Hard* or anything with with Arnold Schwarzenegger in it. The thing is, I understand this isn't gonna float everyone's boat, and I'm okay with that. It's not like I'm all the time twisting Irene's arm to sit there with an extra large box of jujubees whoopin' and hollerin' every time Arnold twists someone's head off. Somewhere along the line, though, Irene got it into her melon that if I would just sit through a few of those tear-jerkers with her, I'd suddenly have some kind of religious experience and we'd both be the better for it. I'm not hard to get along with, but I gotta tell ya, I really don't like that stuff. It creeps me out, but Reeny, she won't get off it.

So anyway, we were on the highway heading up north and Irene was hiding in this book of short stories, and she suddenly goes to squealing and carrying on and just cannot believe what she has come across. She finally calms down enough to tell me she has read a story about Regular Ernie. (I gotta interrupt myself here and tell you what she really said. She said that she read a story about "Regular." Geez, that bugs me. The man's name is Regular Ernie. What's so hard about that? It must be a guy thing, because the only people who have a problem with it are the wives. I've tried to make Irene understand that you just cannot go around calling a grown man "Regular." It's not like Ernie is his last name. I hope she never meets a Navy man who is a Rear Admiral.)

It turns out that some guy named Ray Carver has written a short story about going to visit a friend in some drying-out place and that guy happened to be a chimney sweep. To me, it's an interesting coincidence that we are going to visit such a person in such a place and on the way there read a story about going to visit such a person in such a place. To Irene, however, it is *profound.* It is not profound enough, however, to make me forget about last weekend.

That's the part I was saying I'm not so hot to talk about, but I will say this: the whole thing centers around Irene and this silly rabbit friend of hers—Carmine, who's had so much peroxide soaked into her empty skull over the years that she's bleached out about a trillion brain cells. They set up this shindig that has to do with Carmine's big-deal boyfriend and I still don't understand why we had to be there, but Irene says this is her best friend and she needs us and why can't I do this one thing and wah, wah, wah, and all right, so I'll go already. Geez. (Remember George Gobels' famous line: Did you ever feel like the world was a tuxedo and you were a pair of brown shoes?)

So anyway, we went over to Carmine's for dinner, and I'll admit, at first it wasn't bad. It was really quite a spread. There was a lot of that fancy stuff those gay chefs get all excited about and love to show off the correct pronunciation of. It was pretty tasty, though, and since Carmine the Intellectual had hocked her mother's jewelry to pay for it, I figured I might as well chow down. Then comes the movie. That's the part I told you earlier I wasn't crazy to talk about, and I will remind you that I have already asked you not to crowd me on that, thank you very much.

All I'm saying is that Regular Ernie carries a lot of stuff around, and the way he is, he has to *think* about everything. Spend a couple decades trying to figure out things that just don't make sense any kind of way and you'll start hitting the bottle yourself. To tell you a lot more than you really need to know, I will let it slip here that I know Regular Ernie well enough to know that it hurt him deep inside to be inflicting so much grief on Gladys when the whole drinking thing got out of control. Being a thinker, Regular Ernie knew he needed some help getting a grip on things. So now here we are, going up to visit him in the drying-out place.

When we got up there, you could tell that Regular Ernie was happy for the company. He tells us this place is the Blue Collar Betty Ford Clinic and should be called The Center for the Advancement of Hope Over Reality. That Regular Ernie kills me. Then he and Reeny got into this heavy philosophical discussion that lost me completely. Reeny had come bouncing through the door babbling about the Ray Carver story and wouldn't give the man a moment's peace until he sat right down and read the damn thing. I'm sitting there tapping my toes waiting for him to finish up and tell Irene, yes, this is very nice, thank you for sharing. (Oh yeah, that's another thing. Regular Ernie is not only smart, he's polite. Always has been.) But no, he buys right into it. Not as excitedly as Irene (guys like me and Regular Ernie, we don't get excited) but you can tell they're sharing a wavelength.

Regular Ernie says he's across town from Easy Street but at least he has a bus token. (Regular Ernie talks like that. He just kills me). I gotta tell you, though, he's got a better shot at staying sober than those other door-knobs I seen stumbling around there. On a good day they could maybe get work holding up lamp posts somewhere. Anyway, what Regular Ernie has come to realize, he tells us, is that he isn't fighting an over-whelming urge to drink, but is actually losing his reasons for feeling compelled to drink. Much like the guy in the story.

In case you haven't read Ray Carver's *Where I'm Calling From*, let me put it in a nutshell for you. This guy is a chimney sweep who, as a kid, fell down into a dry well and laid there for a long time, which was a big deal and apparently affected his psyche. He later became a chimney sweep with a drinking problem and ended up drying out and had hope for himself because he was thinking about getting out of the business altogether. It's a good story and Ray Carver is a first-rate writer. I take nothing away from the man, but you should've heard what Irene and Regular Ernie do with this story.

Regular Ernie says that yes, there is an analogy here. "Ever look up a chimney?" he asks. "What is it but a narrow well? What is more 'down' than the bottom of a well? But," Regular Ernie says, "there is blue sky and sunshine available if you will just look up." That whole where-there-is-life-there-is-hope thing. His experience in the well touched Old Boy in that place we all have (actually, he said in that *masochistic* place we all have, but that kind of talk makes me uncomfortable) that loves to be ter-rorized.

Irene says, "*Exactly,*" and goes on to explain to Regular Ernie that spending a couple of years terrorizing himself crawling through tunnels under the jungle did the same thing to him. She says that *metaphorically* (ever since she became a literary genius, Irene loves words like that),

Regular Ernie was trying to recapture that experience by sticking his head into people's fireplaces, but it has actually had the opposite and therapeutic effect of desensitizing him by impressing on him that there is no danger there. Not only that, but every time Regular Ernie looked up a chimney (you could tell this was the cherry on top for Irene), he saw the light at the end of the tunnel, which is what he had been looking for all along. Therefore, the urge to put his life on the line has petered out entirely, hence his recent decision to get out of that line of work entirely. (At this point I may have been gagging ever so slightly.)

Reeny eats this up like candy. Now they are analyzing the phenomenon of Regular Ernie being a tunnel rat and then later on, turning into a chimney sweep. They figure they are really onto something here. I don't say anything but, hey, I've personally been inside a few of those tunnels and I never once saw a freaking fireplace.

After a long and intense discussion about Regular Ernie's personal inner workings and such, he and Reeny conclude, you understand, that an important breakthrough has occurred. That's what they say. Me? I say it's possible to dig too deep. But then, what do I know? I thought *Sophie's Choice* was a race horse.

The hell of it is, Irene knew that's what I was thinking because I commented on the kinds of names they give those racing nags when I saw the video cassette sitting there on top of Carmine's idiot box when we came in. She could have given me some warning. All of a sudden I'm in this situation (I'll spare you the whys and wherefores; believe me, it was one of those situations) where, if I just up and leave, I'm the clod who threw a wet blanket on the evening, just when Carmine needed us to be there for her. So I suffered through it. And believe me, I suffered. I am still suffering. Do you know what this choice is Sophie had to make? Why do they make movies like that? This is entertainment? When we leave there, I'm pissed. Irene thinks the movie was beautiful. I tell her—that's beauty, how about we get a couple of flame-throwers and take out a nursery school? Cripes, that'll be so freaking beautiful they'll have to bring Leonardo back from the Great Beyond to capture it all on a chapel ceiling somewhere.

Soon as we get home, I knock back a couple shots of Jose Cuervo and catch the late news. (Cowboys lost to Philly, just to cap off a perfect evening. Thanks, you bums, now I owe that lardass Fat Mike a sawbuck I can't spare.) I don't got too much to say to the missus and she hits the sack. Turns out I'm up all night with heartburn and other gastrointestinal distress I won't get too specific about, which you should thank me for. Turns out I was over there eating frogs and snails—octopus! for criminy sake—and who knows what other abominations God never intended a normal person would just up and put into his mouth on purpose. No wonder they call that stuff by names only some foreigner can understand.

Bright and early next a.m., mushbrain Carmine calls to say that she and the fag boyfriend have decided to call it quits, and can I come over Saturday to fix her radiator. Reeny says sure.

Sometimes I don't like Irene very much.

WAR STORY

'm hiding out in my shop in the basement right now while Irene is upstairs with a couple of her sisters. This is my sanctuary and, really, my favorite place in the world. I'm never as content as when I'm down here by myself. I would rather sit down here and bang away on this old Royal (five dollar yard sale special) than go to town on that fancy computerized machine of Irene's—just because it's down here. Irene knows this is my space and always knocks and asks permission to enter before coming down the stairs. It's all kind of tongue-in-cheek; she would really be hurt to know that, as a matter of fact, I would rather *nobody* ever came down here. Being alone with my thoughts, keeping my hands busy, is not a luxury for me. I *need* some space occasionally.

I'm proud of what I built down here. Everything has a story to it. A guy like me don't have toys like this without some effort. Took me a lifetime to put this baby together. That drill press? You think I could just run right out and buy something like that? Even used? I wish. Back when Jimmy Carter was president, we had us a big fire down at the shop. A whole section was wiped out. I saw them drag that joker out during the clean up and haul it to the city dump, and I made a beeline out there as soon as I punched out. Took me and two other guys to wrestle it into the back of my truck, them telling me the whole time I was nuts. Spent a couple weeks cleaning and scraping just to get it to the point where I could take it apart. All the wiring was melted and fused together, and the smaller gears were melted and warped, but the big moving parts were pretty much intact. I got on this Royal and wrote the company begging for information, harassed everyone I knew who had any knowledge of these things, went to estate sales and swap meets and junk yards scrounging parts, spent a million fruitless and frustrating hours fighting with the damn thing, and even took the Lord's name in vain a few times. Ate up the best part of two years, but the bottom line: hey, I got me a state-of-the-art drill press and I love it. Stuff like that don't come easy when every nickel counts.

I got me a nice lathe—older than me and you have to switch belts by hand to alter the speed, but it works like a champ. Buncha other stuff, I won't bore you. I'm just saying, this is my little kingdom. When the rest of the world is trying to make me feel small, this is where you'll find me.

You know, I don't just putz around down here. I make some nice stuff. I graduated from bird feeders and spice racks back when the kids was little. That was when I believed my job on the loading dock was a temporary thing and this here is what I would be doing for a living. What happened? Don't ask. Life, that's what. Skinned knees and braces, and mortgages, and birthday after birthday, all shooting by while I was down here dreaming about something a whole lot fancier. I got some ideas on what I can do down here to supplement whatever peanuts we got coming in after they toss me that gold watch. That time is a lot closer now than I had ever imagined it would be.

So you're wondering what I'm hiding from down here today. Irene's sisters, that's what. It looks like I went and did it again. They are always on the lookout for something to ridicule me about and I am never shy about giving them ammunition. Irene doesn't let them get too carried away with it, but she laughs, too, sometimes. The Five Eye Monster has yet to forgive me for Irene marrying down. (Oh, yeah, the monster thing is my little joke. I'm the only one who enjoys it. Are you ready for this? Six sisters and they all have a name that begins with "I." I refer to the gang of them as the "Six I's," or, without Irene, as the Five Eye Monster.) The worst of them is Iris. This is a big girl we are talking about here. She takes her job as Big Sister very seriously, which I have always assumed was the reason she decided to become so huge. Irene was supposed to be the big success story of the family, the first one out of that clan to go off to college and make something of herself. Instead she up and marries some slob with a juvenile record who works on a loading dock. You can imagine the drill—our kids turned out pretty good, that's because of Irene. Our lawn died, that's because of me. Mostly I don't care because I live in my own little world a lot of the time. I got stuff going on they couldn't imagine.

What happened recently, Isabel (I think of her as "i," or "Small I" for being the youngest, and naturally, the smallest one of the bunch) ended up with some kind of fancy perfume her gay son-in-law smuggled back from Paris. This stuff costs something like three hundred seventy-five bucks for five-eights of an ounce at Saks Fifth Avenue, and the I's are going bananas over it. Irene is by far the most down-to-earth of the batch, and even she is wishing that just once she could have a "totally frivolous luxury" of this kind. Needless to say, I don't get it. As far as that goes, Irene isn't gonna get it either, because in this house, that kind of bread is serious business and I got news for a whole truck load of I's: that stuff don't smell that good.

Pretty much all I got that is mine exclusively is what is in my head. I got stuff up there I have never shared with anybody. Irene would bet her life that she knows everything there is to know about me, has heard all my stories, knows everything I've done in life and how I feel about it. Some things I don't talk about. They all know I was in the war. At that time, G.I. life insurance was twenty grand. Iris already had the money spent and my selfishness in not making that amount payable is another inexcusable transgression I have never been forgiven for. They have no idea. I was in the worst of it. The war for me was up close and personal. I ended up as part of a small outfit connected to Special Forces. In reality, it was a pretty shadowy operation. I don't think there was ever much in writing about us. Since almost nobody survived, it's never been an issue. I'm not John Wayne or anything, just someone uniquely suited to do a job that needed doing. I became qualified for this work in part by growing up dirt poor in a home where, often as not, there was nothing to eat if someone didn't go out into the woods and kill something. Miss enough meals and you become a pretty good rifle shot. Beyond that, the major qualifications for this kind of assignment were being able to be alone in a scary place for extended periods of time, and extreme patriotism. Oh, yeah, and be willing to die trying. I was young, what did I know?

When nobody was looking, I took a big, healthy whiff of this big deal perfume, and I gotta tell ya, I was unimpressed. I like the stuff on Irene's dresser a whole lot better. Even so, it's not a good feeling to have your wife wishing she could have something you will never be able to provide, so I went shopping. I can't imagine where these know-it-all broads been buying their perfume, but the first place I stop, they got this real nice-smelling stuff right out on the counter, costs $4.95 for about a quart and a half. I snapped it up.

So now you know why I am once again the subject of a lot of snickering and giggling. I know Irene: every once in a while she'll pour a shot of it down the drain to make it look like she is actually using it and I will pretend to think she really is. And for the next six months or so, Iris will take every opportunity to ask Irene whatever is that lovely scent she is wearing whenever I am within earshot. That's okay. If someone took Irene away from me, I would be upset, too, and it would go deeper than catty remarks.

A year or so back, Irene bought me a T-shirt that said "Crank It Up!" across the front. She figured I'd like it because she knows the kind of fishing I do involves crank bait and I watch this show on ESPN every Saturday morning that is sponsored by a crank bait manufacturer and I am always oohing and aahing over their latest toy. What Irene doesn't know is that "crank" is what bikers call methamphetamine, or speed, and that "cranking up" refers to sticking a needle in your arm and mainlining that poison. The design on the front of the shirt is actually a syringe with a bunch of biker logos and a big marijuana leaf superimposed over the mess of it. It's cleverly done—if you don't look closely and know what to look for, it could be anything. I shudder to think what kind of establishment she bopped into to pick up this little gem. I never enlightened her on it. I've got it folded up and put away. Irene thinks I'm saving it for a special occasion.

What we're going through right now is like the clock thing last year. I'll just give you the punch line: I bought a lamp that is actually a hula girl with a grass skirt and a clock in her tummy. It's cute. Well, it's cute to me, and I guess that's all that matters, because she lives with me now down here in my shop. Now that Irene has her new perfume, I won't have to listen to Iris telling her that the light in our living room isn't too good and she should have me pick up a new table lamp. A real card, that Iris.

If you know me, you know I don't tell war stories. There are a lot of people who know me, don't even realize I was over there. I think about it a lot, though. I mean, it was so *deep*. That whole oriental thing. There was just something in the air. It seemed magical sometimes. The death and horror of it aside, I saw things and had experiences that just weren't normal. Our little outfit went into places where people had never seen Caucasians before, had no notion of a place called the United States, or the war itself, for that matter. It was just a part of life that, without warning or explanation, soldiers came through occasionally and killed people. To them it was like tornadoes or earthquakes or what have you—just a natural phenomenon. The way they accepted it, though, always made such an impact on me. You hear these new-agers talk about somebody being a very old soul. That's how those people struck me. Ageless. There was something in them that was so strong it terrified me. I'll break my rule and tell you one story, but I won't be taking any questions, okay?

We choppered in over this little village in one of those neighboring countries the President of the United States swore we never penetrated. Our mission at the moment was to locate a particular piece of Soviet hardware Intelligence had reason to believe was being field tested in this area. (I'm being a bit vague on the details here because, dumb as it is, much of what we did is still classified under the National Security Act and it would be a felony for me to discuss it.) We weren't looking for a fight, and honestly didn't expect one, but as we were circling low over this little group of huts, all of a sudden a long burst of machine gun fire pours out of one of them. Our door gunner was hit and fell over, so I grabbed the fifty cab (.50 caliber mounted machine gun—in case you don't know, a weapon that fires large projectiles with great rapidity), and poured about a ton of lead into that little hut. After that, we preceded to chop up the local real estate pretty thoroughly, which appeared to take that nasty urge to fight right out of them.

We put down and I ran over to that hut to see if there was anything of interest there. Intelligence gathering was a big part of what we did, especially in these remote areas. What kind of weaponry they had, what may have been on the bodies in terms of maps or orders, or ID, generally paper work of any kind. Inside the doorway was a pile of hamburger laying across an AK 47, which I assumed represented the earthy remains of that misguided individual who had opened fire on us. Beyond him, lying on the floor, was an old woman. She was absolutely tiny, and looked to me to be the oldest individual who had ever lived. There was an enormous hole through her solar plexus, the kind a .50 caliber bullet makes; I could see the dirt floor through it. She turned her head and looked at me. This is the part where I run out of words. You might think that once something is black, it cannot be any blacker. Like, what could be blacker than a bottle of black ink? This woman's eyes were so black they were a color beyond black. Those eyes were bottomless. If I had stumbled over and fell into them, I would still be falling. And the hole through her chest, through a big chunk of spine—there was no blood, no gore, and she was still alive.

Beyond that, what struck me was the incredible beauty of this tiny old woman. What was beautiful about her? I don't know, but that was how she struck me then, and that is how I have always remembered her: very, very old and very, very beautiful. The fact that I had just punched a hole through her little body hit me with all the impact of the bullet I had fired. I lifted her up – I've picked up wet blankets that weighed more – and laid her down on a sleeping mat in the corner. I was trying to make her comfortable, searching for a way to ask her to forgive me, when she shook her head, reached out with both hands and held my face so that I had to look directly into those eyes.

You know how they say your whole life flashes before your eyes when you die? That's what happened here, except that it was her life, and I was watching it in her eyes. I saw her being born to parents disappointed at not getting a son, given away into marriage at a young age, having children and grandchildren and watching them all die over the years. I saw a lifetime of hardship, year after year of mind-numbing labor just to survive—but also the ability to draw great joy from the smallest sources. She carried memories of special moments in the jungle, being surprised by a particularly pretty flower where none had been before, happening upon a pair of newborn tiger cubs, bathing under a waterfall in light filtered through a rainbow; natural wonders that made her feel personally blessed and enormously grateful. For prolonged periods of her life, the only food she knew was boiled rice, but in her mouth rice burst with flavor and was no less a delight than the most demanding gourmet experiences in the world's finest restaurants. She could close her eyes and relive the utter delight of that exotic treat called chocolate given her by a French soldier decades before.

I saw her grow old and come to be regarded as wise and highly respected by all who knew her. Over all, it had been a long, hard road, but she saw it as a good life. Now it was time for it to end, and that was by no means a bad thing, just another step in the natural order. She gave me all that by way of saying that no transgression had occurred, and no forgiveness was necessary. She was ready to move on and wished me well on my life's journey.

I sat there holding her hand, too awestruck to move; eventually it dawned on me that it was very quiet outside. I folded her hands over the hole in her chest, which never bled, and stepped outside. I was alone.

It was weeks before I got the story. The rest of the unit had encountered a guerrilla band drawn by the commotion and had engaged in what is termed a "high intensity exchange," and had high-tailed it out of there, retreating under heavy fire. I was oblivious to it all. A pitched battle with machine gun fire, mortar rockets and a fifty-caliber machine gun going on around me and I didn't hear a sound. A Huey helicopter roaring to life and lifting off just yards away from me and I didn't notice. Enemy guerrillas all around combing the area, and somehow they didn't see me. You explain it. I can't. How long was I in the little hut? Minutes? Hours? Days? It felt like five minutes, but when I came out, there was no one in sight, and it was nearly sundown.

I knew from experience that they didn't lift off without making a serious effort to locate me or my remains, and I knew there would be Search and Rescue spotters out in full force, but at that point I was on my own.

57

I spent the next several weeks trekking through enemy territory at night so I could navigate by the stars, eating monkey meat and generally doing my best to recall basic survival training. Eventually I linked up with an Army long range reconnaissance team and they took me home with them. But all that is just another war story. I won't bore you.

Anyway, we were talking about Iris. Sometimes people ask why I take so much crap from that girl. I dunno. I guess in the overall scheme of things, Iris just isn't that big a deal.

SECTION 2:
INSIDE THE WALLS

THE CRACKER JACKS MAN

I can't imagine how you heard that old story about the cackles, but yeah, that was me. At this stage of the game, what's the point of denying it? I don't usually tell prison stories but hey, you want cackles, I'll give you cackles.

These "local color" stories are hard to tell because there is so much background you need to know for any of it to make sense. As far as the joint goes, I'm gonna be the first convict who ever gave anybody the straight poop. No kidding. Like I said, what do I care? First, take everything you know "for sure" about prison—everything you've read, seen on TV, or generally accept as a given. Bunch it all up together and hit the Delete key. Forget about it. Everything You Know Is Wrong.

Prison populations are made up of goofs, geeks, dope fiends, baby rapers, and psychopaths. Ain't nobody in here for doing something clever (the academic average for the whole system is third grade, okay?) and there's no honor among thieves. That thing in the movies where someone is found out to be a snitch and is instantly dispatched? Give me a break. If there is a stabbing on the yard, the real danger is that you will be trampled by the stampede to see who can get to the captain and be the first to tell. When you read stories in the paper about some crackhead beating his great-grandmother to death for the change in her pocket, or some atrocious sex crime involving children, hey, those are the people who go to prison. Those dashing, devilishly suave criminals you see on the silver screen are actors.

This little tale takes place in Jackson, Michigan, which is the largest walled prison in the world. Altogether, there are over five thousand inmates. This institution is comprised of "inside the walls," and "Trustee Division." T.D. is comprised of "the blocks," two cell blocks just outside the walls, and the five farms that are located several miles from the main prison. That's the place to be. Those guys out there can get all kinds of stuff, even liquor. Hell, you can just up and walk away if you want to. On one of these farms, they raise chickens, which provide eggs and Sunday dinner for the whole enchilada. Guys in T.D. come inside for medical, dental, and certain other needs that T.D. is not equipped to deal with.

So one day I see this kid in the infirmary that had recently transferred to the chicken farm and was lovin' it. He went to telling me about this stuff they call "cackles," which is the additive they mix in the chickens' feed that makes the eggshells tougher to reduce breakage in transport. Somebody got the bright idea to mix a spoon of this in a cup of coffee and drink it. (You really got to wonder, don't you?) It turns out, this stuff will make you high as a witch doctor. These clowns out there are getting zonked on this stuff every day. Kinda guy I was back in those days, my immediate response was "Gimmie some." The kid told me he had a partner who was a truck driver out there, who delivered supplies to where I worked. He said he would send me in some by this dude.

I was working grounds maintenance at that time. All fertilizers, fuel for the mowers, poisons, and so on were stored outside the walls for security reasons and brought inside in small amounts, as needed. I'm looking for this dude to slip me maybe an envelope with a couple shots in it so I can cop a buzz and go on about my business. I'm telling you I almost freaked when we're unloading our supplies and the guy slaps a twenty-five pound bag and says, "This is from Packy."

The ground maintenance building is called the "grounds shack," but it's really a very large building filled with all kinds of junk. There must be a hundred or so bags of different things lying around, been there for years. It was easy to just stash this in the mess. I scooped up a coffee cup full to take back to my cell and tried a spoon. I gotta tell ya, it was okay.

Sort of like speed, but it made your face feel all fuzzy and set off a vibrating sensation all over. Not bad at all, really. I flagged down a couple of the regulars and turned them on to a shot, and pretty soon everyone was clamoring for more. Within an hour, a spoon was selling for five bucks, and there was no keeping up with demand.

The language in prison is really interesting. Somebody should do a study. For no reason I can imagine, this stuff was immediately being referred to as "cracker crumbs." Several other names popped up here and there, but the most widely used label was "Cracker Jacks." A five-dollar package was a "sack."

Cracker Jacks was an overnight sensation. Nobody knew I had twenty-five pounds of it. I had three partners that I was real tight with and I provided them all with an eight-ounce scoop for a hundred bucks each, which allowed them to get zipped (and stay that way), and make a lot of money. Once they got rolling, they were coming to me several times a day for another eight ounces and had a network of guys working under them. In the meantime, I was selling sacks as fast as I could put them together. As far as anyone knew, I was just one of many out there slinging sacks of this stuff.

Pretty soon, I've got more money than I've ever had in my life. Institutional money is called "script"and made in a form similar to poker chips, in the amounts of dimes, quarters and dollars. I had seven large coffee cans full of dollars. I had over one hundred cartons of cigarettes under my bed, twelve really nice leather coats. I had guitars, jewelry, radios, canned food and munchies that wouldn't quit. There were five different guys keeping stuff for me in their cells. I told them chow down on the food, just don't hurt me too bad on the other stuff. In this situation it is understood—the guy is gonna steal a little or he's gonna steal a lot. As long as no one disappeared with everything I gave him, I was happy. I never knew how much these guys helped themselves to because I didn't even keep track of what I gave them. It was all gravy. I had stuff stashed all over the grounds shack, and was giving away groceries and whatever to these old guys who had nothing. All this, and I had barely made a dent in the stash. Absolutely everybody in town was buzzing on this junk. You never saw such happy maniacs.

If you're familiar with the convict mentality, you know what happened next. Not to put too fine a point on it: everything turned to shit. Instead of mixing a spoonful and quietly enjoying the pleasant sensation, those goofs starting taking like ten spoons at a time. Some of them started mixing Cracker Jacks with Valium, a mix referred to as a "CJ & V." There were others mixing it with the traditional institution favorite, fermented anything. Heroin addicts at that time were shooting a concoction of Talwin and Valium (known as Teddys and Bettys), which provides a rush similar to heroin. Their new thing was to drink a Mintzes Mixer (named for Warden Mintzes)—a Cracker Jacks and hooch cocktail—followed up by shooting some Teddys and Bettys. And who knows what the hell else? All of a sudden, those knuckleheads are dropping like flies. It all went off the Stupidity Index one Sunday when three guys died and nine were in the psych clinic under heavy sedation. They carried a van-load of bozos down to U of M hospital for kidney dialysis, and I don't know how many turned yellow and learned that, for all intents and purposes, they no longer had a liver.

While all this is going on, one of my partners got beat up and robbed in a blind spot over behind the kitchen. He was so busted up, he has never recovered all the sight in his right eye. Over a few teaspoons of this junk that makes eggs more transportable. Next thing you know, some guy gets stabbed over a spoon; another guy, for criminy sake, mainlines some of this crap, and spends the last five minutes of his life screaming in agony and vomiting blood. It gets stupider by the day. I cut off the source, but by this time there was so much in circulation, the supply continued throughout the week. As it began getting scarce, the violence increased. These idiots were killing each other over this stuff. Do you understand what I am telling you? You got a spoonful of chicken feed additive that makes you high, and someone will jam a screwdriver through you heart and take it. What's wrong with this picture?

By this time, the administration is frantic. They don't know what the hell is going on. They lock down the whole joint and bring in cops from other institutions, as well as State Police sniff dogs, to do an inch-by-inch, fine-tooth-comb search of the entire facility and everyone in it. It took a large truck to haul off all the weapons they found; you'd be amazed at all the other weird stuff that turned up (that's a story in itself, believe me), but as I could've told them, they found zip regarding cracker jacks. They don't even know what they're looking for.

I was ready at that point to never come within a country mile of that stuff ever again. Or at least for a long time. As far as I was concerned, I had enough to live like a king for the next couple years, and if the need arose, I could always very quietly put a few sacks out to a selected clientele without raising a ruckus. Life is never that simple in jail. One of the clowns I put to work got involved with these bad dudes slinging heroin. In the end—even with as much money as we were making, you understand—he somehow owes them a small fortune. I got him begging me to come up with some more or these guys will kill him. (I know these guys. This is a serious threat.) This other goofball went bananas with a couple bookies and he ended up in debt for a king's ransom. All of a sudden, he's making sounds that suggest his only way out may be to roll over on me. I gave both of them twelve ounces to get straight and make then understand this was The End. They turned this over to the people they owed, who immediately sacked it and picked up where we left off. A spoon is about one gram; there are twenty-eight grams in an ounce. I just put a fresh twenty-four ounces out there. You do the math.

At this point, we got a full blown crisis. The guys selling this stuff don't care about squat except getting rich as soon as possible before it plays out. They started cutting the stuff to stretch it, and didn't care what they cut it with. Rat poison was no different than powdered sugar. It was time to get out of Dodge. I put in a request for transfer to Marquette, which is way the hell and gone up in the Upper Peninsula. That was a radical step. Nobody wants to go to Marquette. Transfer there is usually for disciplinary reasons. As prisons go, that one ain't much fun. I gave the classification clerk my best leather jacket and two cartons of Pall Malls to make sure it happened. I was scheduled for the next bus.

There is quite a lot of "green money"—regular U.S. currency—in circulation in Jackson, although it is contraband and will be confiscated if found. Green money is quite valuable. In normal times, a fifty dollar bill is worth seventy-five dollars in script. A hundred dollar bill goes for as much as one hundred and seventy-five dollars. Think about it. There is only so much you can do with script. Green money you can make deals with cops to bring you stuff in, send it home, hire a lawyer, etc. I was pay-ing top dollar for all the green I could get my hands on, and sending it out to a Christian girl I knew who offered to open a bank account and deposit it for me. The leather coats went out to different people as gifts; liquidating my assets became a full time job.

I made a deal with this old Arab guy who wanted to buy a hundred cartons of cigarettes for ten dollars each. I had done business with him in the past and I knew he was straight, so I gave him the cigarettes. He was on his way to the telephone to call his wife and tell her where to send my money, when these three dope fiends blindsided the old guy and robbed him. He made it to the infirmary, but died that night. Later, Ali. Good-bye, thousand bucks. A couple days before the Marquette transfer, there was a major shakedown in Eight Block. Three cops shook down my cell and had a field day.

Any amount of script over ninety-five dollars is considered contra-band. They counted out ninety-five of them jokers and left me a receipt for the other seven hundred and seventy. There are also limits on cloth-ing, cassette tapes, and the like. Any jewelry, other than a wedding band with no stone and a watch of less than fifty dollars value, is contraband. The guys holding loot for me were likewise hit hard. Say it this way, I lost a lot of stuff. Those rules are designed to discourage the kind of hustling that results in the kind of wealth I had accumulated. The kind of wealth I had accumulated indicated that I was involved in something not entirely kosher. If I hadn't already been classified for Marquette, I could at that point have reasonably expected to be classified for Marquette.

The losses didn't really bother me because, hey, I'm the Cracker Jacks Man. My last day there, I scooped up seven pounds of that stuff and stashed it away in my property. The remainder stayed right where it was. Chances are good I'll be back this way before all is said and done. That was money in the bank.

After arriving in Marquette, I got with a couple old heads I knew and ran the situation down on them. My proposition is this: you guys hold onto this stuff, get high as much as you want, but don't sell any. You want something from the commissary, let me know, and I've got you covered. Let me be the one and only person here selling this stuff so I can keep things quiet and under control. I'll do this in such a way that outside of a chosen few, no one will even know this stuff is in town.

Life is never that simple in jail. Turns out, the one guy was a real goof. He couldn't resist the chance to make a buck and play the role of drug kingpin. He had the smallest amount, which was sixteen ounces in a Jergen's lotion bottle, but hey, do the math. That's a bunch of dope. He ounced it out, and it was gone by the time I knew anything. Next thing you know, the yard looks like a gladiator school and the administration is freaking. I'll say this for myself: I'm always thinking. This brainstorm hit me like the solution to all my earthly problems.

I stopped the captain and told him to put me together with the deputy warden, and I can solve all this cracker jacks foolishness before lunch. Ten minutes later I was sitting across the desk from The Man, who said only, "I'm all ears." My rap was simple. Cracker jacks is in Marquette; none of us wants a repeat of what happened in Jackson. I am in a unique position to stop it. I will bring to you, and place on your desk, every last crumb of that stuff that exists in this institution—and I can promise you we're talking no less than six pounds—and guarantee you that it will not resurface. I will give up no names or any other information, but I will stop this scourge once and for all. In a very deadpan voice, the dep responded, "And all this you will do as a service to humanity."

"No," I responded, "All this I will do for a parole."

The dep flipped open my file and went over my particulars. They ain't pretty. It's the damnedest thing, really. On paper, I look like a real desperado, but in reality, I'm not such a bad guy. I mean, I'm not dangerous, and there is a long list of people I won't steal from. Those who know me say I am generous to a fault, and I can be a million laughs. Right now I am doing thirty-five years for a bank robbery in which shots were exchanged with the police. That is what is known as "aggravating circumstances." They get aggravated when you have a Hollywood-style shootout with the cops in downtown traffic. What can I say? I was scared. Nobody was hurt.

I also have a juvenile record for fleeing and eluding police in a stolen vehicle and escaping from a detention facility in Kentucky. I have adult arrests for cocaine (twice), and this really unpleasant thing that had to do

67

with a piece of jewelry they found on me that was last seen on a corpse in a funeral home. Aggravated circumstances, roughly translated, means, "This dude gets no breaks." The dep looked at me over the top of his glasses and said, "A parole. You're a comedian, right?" I asked him if he thought all those corpses littering the yard downstate were a skit from *Saturday Night Live*. He said he would get back with me.

I left out of there really depressed. That guy treated me like I was some kind of chump, just when I was feeling clever about myself. "Don't call me, I'll call you." Right.

I spent the rest of the week laying in my cell, not thinking about anything, just chilling out. The yard was in chaos. That sixteen ounces of cackles had those fools going berserk. When I heard that this kid from Grand Rapids had died, I was just sick. I did time with his dad back when we were both in juvie; he gave me my first tattoo. I gathered up every last crumb of that stuff that was still stashed away and flushed it into nonexistence. Gone forever. Good riddance. Finis.

Bright and early next morning, I was summoned to the deputy's office. He gave me a cup of coffee and sat down. "Well," he said, "it took some doing, but word came this morning directly from the governor's office: I am ordered to get that stuff off the yard. If you can hold up your end of it, we can start processing your release papers. How much of that stuff can you bring me?"

That was nineteen years ago. I've been here in Marquette ever since. When I couldn't deliver, they took a closer look at me and found out about all the money and stuff that was confiscated from me in down in Jackson. The coincidence that cracker jacks showed up in Marquette at about the same time as I did was not overlooked. They confiscated everything I had except a toothbrush and a bar of soap and gave me a statement saying this was "suspected drug proceeds" and would be returned to me if their investigation cleared me. I don't know how much of an investigation there was, but apparently I was never cleared.

The girl I sent all those hundred dollar bills to apparently moved without leaving a forward. Things got tight there for me for a while. I don't brood on stuff like that. I figger, that's life. You got your ups and you got your downs. I have been through a hundred scams and hustles since then. Right now I'm thinking, I know this guy who works in the treatment plant out in T.D. here. I figure: I can tie a line to a handball and flush that sucker; he can fish it out on that end, attach a package of dope and I can haul it back in. I can cop a buzz, maybe make a few bucks. . . .

A JACKSON TALE

The first time I saw a guy get killed, it really wigged me out. The most succinct thing I can tell you is that it is not like you see on T.V. I was unprepared for how nauseating it was. This big guy named Bama lit into some biker dude with a screwdriver. The guy was wearing a heavy leather jacket and Bama had to hit him hard to penetrate it. The sound was like hitting a side of beef with a ball bat, and then pulling it back out, kind of a sucking sound. Thunk . . . shhee, thunk . . . shhee. Bama was being very deliberate, almost casual about it, his expression one of total concentration. Thunk . . . shhee. I won't be so tacky as to give you a blow by blow account of the whole thing—it got pretty gross. I just mention that to tell you something about myself. That whole thing made me sick; I was in a very unsettled state for several days after that. That's why it was so weird a few years later when I decided I had to kill a guy.

As I said, I don't like violence. I came up in a bad neighborhood, though, and have spent most of my life in the joint. Violence is no stranger and I can exercise it as necessary. I just don't like it, that's all.

Back in the old days I had a friend named Ray. This man was a killer. Most of his life he had been a professional soldier (the term he preferred over "mercenary"). He had a few stories he told about things that hap-

70

pened in Africa or South America, but they were just interesting anec-
dotes, not blood-and-guts war stories.

The thing I started to tell you about began on a slow winter afternoon
a couple years back. It was real cold and crappy outside. Everyone was
kicked back watching football and just chillin' out. My cell was on fourth
gallery in Eight Block. At halftime, Ray skated up to hang out and we got
to talking about how there was nothing decent for chow that night, so I
volunteered to zip over to the commissary and pick up some munchies
for later on. Ray had a key he had made out of a fork and got my door
open to let me out. Outside the Eight Block door I grabbed a rake and a
big garbage bag to carry as a "skating pass." "Skating" is the term
applied to being someplace without a pass, or otherwise illegally. With a
rake and the proper attitude, I could pretend to be on the grounds crew,
on the job; a cop that normally would have challenged me for a pass now
would barely notice me.

I was halfway to my destination before I realized just how cold it really was. I was trying to stuff my hands in my pockets and still carry the
damn rake, with my head pulled down into my collar, not paying attention—which is always a mistake in Jackson. Before I realized it, I had
strolled into the middle of a snakepit.

Jackson is a society as much as any other town of five thousand.
There are civic leaders and do-gooders, bad guys and gangsters, and
whatever else falls in between. At this time there was a drug kingpin in
town named Mack Street. Not just Mack, or any other variation, but
"Mack Street." His reputation had preceded him long before his arrival in
Jackson. Mack Street was well-known in the Detroit underworld as a
pimp and drug dealer. He was reputed to own the largest "stable" of
prostitutes in the city, all of them drug-addicted and at his mercy. He
delighted in telling tales of his creative sadism. This guy was moving
massive amounts of heroin through Jackson and loved playing the role of
Mr. Big. He owned the only full-length fur maxi coat in the institution. A
couple of wanna-be's had shown up with maxi coats during Mack
Street's reign, but he had sent people to confiscate them. He had his boys
cut them up and sell the material for hobbycraft. Mack Street was con-
stantly surrounded by a team of flunkies. These goofs were born to fol-

low and never had it so good as living off the crumbs Mack Street let fall their way.

The first thing that registered was a pair of green patent-leather platform shoes topped by the gray fur of that famous coat. I looked up into the broad gold-studded smile and malevolent eyes of an individual I had long despised from a distance and knew I was in trouble. The posse crowded around me and there was no help in sight. The smell of alcohol and marijuana still permeated the air. Stoned, bored, wanting to flex their muscles and impress their benefactor, the jackals were just waiting for a sign from their master.

"Whachu doin' on my yard, little ol' White Boy?" Mack Street demanded. Snickering all around. Before I had a chance to verbalize a response, Mack Street's hand snaked out and slapped me. Hard. Not a punch, like he would hit a man, but a slap, such as he would deliver to one of his bitches. Not a blow meant to damage or disable, but a slap, meant to convey contempt, designed to humiliate, to make a statement. To amuse his lapdogs. All of the above he accomplished.

A prison society is so macho it is a parody of machismo. Nothing is more of an insult than a slap. To not spill blood in response is to be identified forevermore by that shortcoming. My reaction was not a reluctant acquiescence to peer pressure, however. It came from deep within and was the most passionate, heartfelt emotion of my life. Never, before or since, have I experienced such pure, all-consuming rage. I drew back to fire, but someone grabbed my hair from behind and jerked me back violently. I lost my balance and went down hard, momentarily stunned when my head hit the asphalt. By the time I regained my senses and got to my feet, they were moving away, laughing, high-fiving each other, and looking around for more mischief. I knew that within minutes I would be forgotten—which intensified the indignity of it all.

That flash of rage I experienced did not recede. As I made my way back to Eight Block, it mounted and grew with each step. By the time I pulled the door open to enter the block, I was operating on something primal. I have never been so dangerous as I was at that time. Nothing mattered but that I kill Mack Street. Getting caught and paying the penalty didn't enter into the equation.

Ray and I both had weapons hidden away in the block where we could get to them in an emergency. He had the baddest blade I had ever seen inside the walls stashed just inside the gate on the third gallery catwalk. It was about eight inches long, sharp on both sides, coming to a fine point. The handle was a separate wooden piece that snapped on when needed. At its broadest point, this joker was almost three inches wide, guaranteed to slice open something important if inserted pretty much anywhere in the human anatomy. I had that baby and was down the first flight of stairs before Ray caught up with me. If I had killed somebody right then, I honestly could have claimed temporary insanity. I was literally crazy with rage. I couldn't register the actual words he was saying to me, only the fact that he stood between me and killing Mack Street. I tried to tell him to get out of my way, but all that came out was an animalistic growl. Then I made the mistake of taking a swing at him.

If you watch *Star Trek* or such things, you know what a time warp is. That's what I experienced. I drew back to fire on Ray, and then I was sort of bent over with my face pushed into the corner of the wall, my right arm raised high behind me. I was howling like a maniac. Suddenly a lightning bolt of pain shot from my wrist and up my arm, which served to draw me through the blazing red fog of madness back to reality—still dangerously angry, but at least in contact with my surroundings. "Boy, you runnin' on eight strong cylinders of Pure Stupid." As the words registered, I realized that Ray had me in one of those fancy martial arts holds that have to do with pinching nerves at critical junctures. I was later chagrined to learn that I was so effectively disabled with only two fingers. "Are you with us now?" he asked. I growled something unintelligible through clenched teeth.

"Nobody's telling you don't do this, whatever the hell this is. But I'm telling you, don't do it stupid." At that point he had me in another one of those two-finger locks that commands instant compliance, and was walking me down to my cell. After kicking my door shut and jamming the lock so I couldn't get back out, he disappeared for a few minutes and came back with a couple joints and a coffee jar of apple jack. Ten minutes later I was calmed down enough to speak in coherent sentences. After hearing the story, Ray said, matter of factly, "You are right, of course. Mack Street must die."

Jackson is a very old institution and has many features not included in the newer, cost-efficient facilities. One of the anachronisms is an auditorium, much like the old movie theater you can find in small towns everywhere. Sometimes performers come in and do live shows, but mostly the auditorium is used for showing third-rate movies on the weekends. Ray was in charge of maintaining the equipment and running the projectors. Having access to the auditorium during the times it was closed gave him a sanctuary most inmates don't have. (Anytime you can be alone in a quiet space in the joint, you have a priceless luxury.) He made arrangements with the captain for me to be detailed to work with him for a week on some pretense, and we went to work training for the hit on Mack Street.

When I reported to my detail the first day, I found that my mentor had constructed a very impressive dummy. "Our objective," Ray explained, "is to be swift, deadly, and silent. If this happens quickly and quietly enough, there will be no credible witnesses. The point is to get away with it. To get busted for this is to trade your life for his, and that means you lost. Only people who have no idea of the reality of it think that such a hit is simple."

The plan was to ambush Mack Street in the theater after a movie, when he was in a crowd. Ray would come up behind him, loop a towel around his throat from behind and lean back, pulling Mack Street off his feet and leaving his torso wide open. This position would also serve to separate his ribs and offer a wider soft spot for my knife, which I would shoot into that space and into his grimy little heart. Sounds simple, don't it?

Ray held the dummy by the towel from behind, and I made my thrust. The tiniest movement on his part made my parry ineffectual. A wounding was total failure. Circumstances would allow no more than a few seconds and one shot at putting that blade where it needed to go. Time and time again we went through the drill. Ray put the dummy through every possible movement and squirm Mack Street might make. I learned where to thrust if he twisted around and presented his side to me, or if I had to go through the back. I practiced where to hit him if he drew up his feet and tried to kick, what to do in the unlikely event that he had some training in this area and knew better than to make the instinctive move of grabbing for the towel around his throat. There were numerous possible variations and we drilled on all of them over and over. At the end of six hours, I was utterly exhausted and quite discouraged. Ray just shrugged. "Nothing is easy," he said.

The second day of drilling went a little smoother. It all began to jell; the weapon felt comfortable and familiar in my hand. I was accustomed to hitting hard with it, not making the amateurish mistake of thinking the weapon would do all the work and just slide in. Day two of drilling was no less exhaustive, but much more gratifying. Days three, four, and five were progressively more satisfying and invigorating. I was obsessed with my mission. It was all I thought about. I did not read my mail, watch T.V., or even get high. When I was not training to kill Mack Street, I was thinking about it. Nothing else mattered.

Finally, the night I was living for arrived. I was wearing a dark blue hooded sweatshirt and state-issue blue pants. I sat in the aisle seat a couple rows behind Mack Street. Ray saw our positions from the projection booth and, after he put the final reel on, he slipped down and sat on the aisle a few rows ahead of Mack Street. As soon as the flick ended and people started moving up the aisle, we would both flip up our hoods, tie them tight around our faces, and make our move. After the hit, we would melt into the crowd, then get back to the block and get rid of any bloody clothing as quickly as possible. It was all coming together.

I had no idea what the film was that night, only that it was the longest movie in history. Finally it was over, and everything was moving according to plan. Mack Street was coming up the aisle, Ray was behind him with his hood up and shades on. I kept my seat, waiting. The towel was out and rising up behind Mack Street's head, and something clicked.

Mack Street's face registered shock, his glance snapped in my direction, and he was suddenly looking me directly in the eye, his expression one of amazement and disbelief, but total revelation. In that moment our eyes held I realized he knew exactly what was about to happen. Mack Street jumped up onto the seat next to him and ran across that section of seats to the aisle on the far side of the room and sprinted to the exit. Understand me, he was stepping on the narrow edge of the back of these theater seats, from one to another, across a section at least thirty-five seats wide. All this in a shot, barely making contact on each step, like a puppet on a string. I was mesmerized and hadn't even stood up yet when Ray was leaning over me, stuffing his towel into the space between two seats and telling me to lose the knife. I dropped it on the floor and we headed back to Eight Block as casually as possible.

I was freaked out. I was asking what happened even as I was describing what happened, and again demanding, "What the hell happened? It was just like he suddenly looked into another dimension and actually saw it happen. He saw it, Ray, he knew! How could that be? What the hell happened in there anyway?"

I gotta say, my partner was pretty cool about it. After I calmed down enough to let him talk he said, "What happened was exactly what you said. He saw it. I've been to some very strange places and I've seen a lot of things. Sometimes events are taken out of our hands. Maybe there was a little angel siting on his shoulder whispering in his ear. Maybe it was God. Hell, maybe it was the Sugar Plum Fairy. I do know this though—Mack Street was not meant to die by your hand, and my advice to you is to forget about bucking up against that. The message here is bigger than both of us."

"God intervened on behalf of Mack Street?" I asked skeptically. "That doesn't work for me." Ray gave me a funny little smile and said, "Sometimes you amaze me with things you understand, and sometimes I'm amazed by what you don't understand."

The buzz on the yard next day was that Mack Street and five of his lieutenants were in segregation per their own request for protection and had made a deal to get transferred to an undisclosed location in exchange for ratting out the cops who were supplying them with drugs. Nobody seemed to know anything about me: neither my original encounter with Mack Street or the thwarted hit.

Ray and I sort of drifted off in different directions after that. We were still friends in that I knew he'd be there if I needed him, and he knew he could count on me. We'd speak sometimes, but the bond had sort of disintegrated. I spent quite a lot of time contemplating matters that had never occurred to me before, and every day I was more grateful that things worked out the way they did.

Several months after that night in the auditorium, I happened to be in the Control Center and saw my old friend there with all his property packed up and realized that he was part of the group being transferred that day. I strolled over, as casually as possible. Where we live a guy can't just say, "Hey man, I thought we were friends. You're going to leave, I will quite possibly never see you again, and you don't even say *adios?*"—although I'm sure that was all over my face.

When Ray saw me he just gave me that funny smile again and shook his head. "You still haven't figured it out, have you?" The transfer sergeant hollered for everyone to grab their stuff and file through the gate. Ray threw his duffel up on his shoulder and headed out. At the gate he paused and looked at me. "Dig. You've been all this time trying to puzzle out how it is that some higher force reached out and saved Mack Street from going down a path that would lead to his destruction. You've got it bass-ackwards. It wasn't Mack Street who was saved from making that mistake. Think about it."

As a matter of fact, I have thought about it. Sometimes I am able to just shrug it off—hey, bizarre things happen in this life. Sometimes I get very philosophical about it. I often find myself thinking thoughts that guys like me don't talk about right out loud.

This is what I know for sure: There has been a prison at Jackson since before Michigan was a state. Many thousands of men have passed through here and they have all had a story to tell. When the dust finally settles and the sun sets on this wretched chunk of real estate for the last time, that thing with me and Mack Street will be just another Jackson tale.

APRIL 10, 1983

T he convict lies on his bed, arms behind his head, staring at the bottom of the bunk above him. To all appearances, he is relaxed, lost in thought. This facade is maintained only with supreme effort. Several times he had to remind himself not to wiggle his toes back and forth in that tell-tale anxious gesture. Year after year of contemplating this evening and it is all unraveling because of one idiot inmate who is convinced he can be pals with some idiot cop. Unreal.

The facility is a minimum security barracks known as "The Farm," although it has been years since it actually functioned in that capacity. Situated several miles from the main prison, it now serves as an overflow for the Trustee Division. The long, low building contains sixty bunk beds, an office for the cops, and not much else. Without fences or other perimeter security, the only impediment to walkaway is the constant bed checks. During the day a bell rings every two hours, at which time all inmates return to their bunks; an officer makes rounds to determine that all are present and accounted for. If they are, normal activity resumes. If not, the missing inmate is paged twice over the P.A. system, after which police are contacted and paperwork is begun to declare him escaped. After dark, this check is made every hour on the hour. Except on Wednesday nights. Wednesday is movies night; a projector is set up to show third-rate movies on the wall of the basement of the chow hall. Most attend, just to break the monotony. Tonight is special: the movie is *Star Wars*, which no one has seen, and everyone is looking forward to. What a break! A count immediately before and immediately after the movie will give him a good two and a half hour head start.

At movie time, the rush for good seats downstairs leaves only two inmates behind. The other one is this idiot in the bunk about ten feet away who immediately flags down this idiot cop and strikes up an idiot conversation about pickup trucks. It evolves from there to deer hunting stories, beer drinking escapades and the whole gambit of redneck interests. They are like twins separated at birth who have suddenly found one another. Strolling to the restroom, behind the cop, and firing his best if-looks-could-kill glare at the idiot several times proves ineffectual. Nothing to do but wait them out. *Star Wars* is well beyond the halfway point when—thank you, Jesus!—the phone rings and Officer Friendly ambles up to the office. His best friend in the world takes this opportunity to visit the restroom. With the Bubba Brothers out of the way, the convict slides open a window behind his bunk and tosses out a fully packed duffel bag and follows it through. The duffel, green canvas Army surplus, is four feet long, twelve inches in diameter, tightly packed, weighing forty pounds. With it strapped across the shoulders, the dynamics of walking become an exercise in controlled chaos.

Within seconds, despite running into what seems like gale force winds, he is in the field beyond the small yard, jogging in the direction of that important rendezvous. Just as his spirits begin to soar, a cold realization strikes like an icicle through his heart. He has forgotten the Frosted Flakes! No! He freezes in a moment of indecision, trying to convince himself to blow it off, but is then running back across the yard, sliding the window open from outside, and scrambling back in. The only thing left in the locker is a small box of Frosted Flakes, which he snatches, jams into a coat pocket, diving back out the window all in one movement. Resuming his trek across the field, he is soon ankle deep in cloying, sucking mud. Fed by melted snow, only a few degrees above zero, the slop is icy cold, penetrating to the flesh. Trudging on, he finds the mud is suddenly knee deep, and then deeper, before he backtracks and strikes out on a path to circumnavigate what turns out to be a bog fifty feet in diameter.

Finally to the woods, and an unpleasant discovery. This leg of the journey was slated to take twenty minutes. What had appeared a short jog across the field to the patch of woods, then a hundred feet or so to the road, was a wildly optimistic illusion. Not woods at all, but a long strip of trees twenty feet wide, followed by a vast expanse of icy swampland. Barbed wire fencing on both sides of "woods," slippery palms savaged climbing over. Push on. Feet throbbing, fingers stinging with cold, ripped palms bleeding copiously. One foot snags in the treacherous grasping mud, trip face first. Up and moving again, mud sucks shoe off and returns it in exchange for wristwatch, completely filled with refrigerated slime, only after prolonged search. On and on, stumbling, mud in eyes, inside clothes, painfully cold, nothing within sight but more of the same. Keep moving. Back up and renegotiate only when ooze is more than waist high, which is often. Stepping backward and falling over from awkwardness of duffel and demonic hands in the mud tugging tenaciously at feet. Suddenly, the wind carries his name and number: he is being paged. *Star Wars* is over, rounds have been made and he is officially missing. That two and a half hour lead time now a grim joke. Within minutes, state and local police informed an escaped convict is wandering the night. His ride has disappeared and he is being sucked into an ocean of ice cream.

No options—stay in motion, nothing distinguishable in the thick inky blackness of the night, all physical sensors screaming in protest. Nothing doesn't hurt, isn't painfully cold, wet, aching or bleeding. Slipping and stumbling in the firm areas, pulling and jerking against grasping goo in soft areas, pushing against nearly solid walls of sludge where it sinks to three feet, four feet, and more; struggling fifteen minutes to gain a short distance, only to backtrack when it threatens to become bottomless. No visible landmarks for reference, all sense of direction lost, just move, hope it's not a big circle.

On the road, a thousand feet away—a million miles, a light year, an eon, a lifetime—a car cruises slowly away from the pickup spot. Running again, such as one runs on frozen feet carrying a heavy duffel through frigid, slippery mud, into a blasting north wind. Trying to shout, but gasping for breath, the convict struggles, slips and falls again, striving to reach the road, knowing his ride will be gone, but knowing, too, that the one absolute guarantee is no good will come of being in this freezing quicksand. Once again, the mud is knee deep and more. He pushes forward anyway and the freezing muddy goop is waist high. No more turning back, he presses on, a slow-motion nightmare. Despair sets in. This was not the plan. Contemplating just dropping and letting archaeologists discover his skeleton in a future millenium, he looks up and sees Hope. His ride, miraculously, making another pass down that distant road. Every bit of energy is summoned and put into rushing onward. The mud does not get deeper, and eventually recedes. He reaches the road at a point the headlights passed moments before. With everything left in him, he screams into the wind, and nearly drops to his knees when brake lights flame to life sixty feet ahead.

As he flops into the van, the driver turns and, with a thick cockney accent, asks, "Where to, then, gov'nor?" "Motown" is the answer, and they both laugh as the driver hands him his first beer in thirteen years. It it delicious.

Not until several years later, over a margarita at a sunny sidewalk cafe in San Miguel de Allende does the chauffeur confide that he had given up on him over an hour earlier and gone home. He was out again later for cigarettes and decided on an impulse to drive up and down that road one last time before returning home.

First stop: a highway rest area just outside of Jackson. Muddy clothing stripped off and discarded. Dressing out of the duffel, reflecting that in his years of talking to scores of inmates returned from escape, he had never known one who took his property with him. "Travel light," they all advised sagely. Not willing to take a lot of escape advice from losers who hadn't succeeded at it, he has carried everything he owned. Not a bad idea after all.

Greyhound bus terminal, Detroit, two hours later: a bearded, slightly disheveled-looking individual with an Army duffel bag and makeshift bandages on his hands strolls to the ticket counter. He rips the top off a small cereal box and extracts the four twenty dollar bills secreted inside. "One way to Toronto, please." The plan is simple, though naive. Procure Canadian birth certificate, join their army, voila! Food, shelter, clothing, and anonymity all in one neat package.

On the bus he smiles, thinking of how clever the cops will feel when they find the letters stashed away that he "accidentally" left behind—particularly the one in Spanish giving him directions to a safehouse in Central America. Had to go through the motions several times to make sure that snitch in the bunk across the way noticed his stash place. He would have reported it by now. Hope he is well rewarded.

All goes well until the bus stops on the Canadian side of Windsor Tunnel. No-nonsense officials demanding picture identification. You don't drive? You have nothing with your name and picture on it? What is your citizenship? Do you understand this is an international border? Who can we call on the phone to vouch for your identity? Why are you trying to enter this country? How is it you have no identification? What happened to your hands? What did you say your name was? What is your social security number? What was your last address? Where were you born? What is the first line of "The Star-Spangled Banner?" Who was the last president of the United States? How is it again you have no identification?

Relentlessly, from several different directions. Just sort of drifting, you know, heard about some work up in Toronto from this chick I met in Cincinnati, I have her phone number . . . thought, why not? You know? Fell down on some broken glass last night. Yeah, I drink a little . . . no driver's license, epileptic . . . just sort of catch day work here and there, you know . . . no family, really, just sort of alone in the world, but I do okay . . . just never thought of Canada as a foreign country, you know, I mean, it's just right there, English speaking people and all . . . they play baseball, right? Empty your pockets right here. All kinds of stuff, a small envelope of aspirin gets intense scrutiny . . . A Mountie pulls the cap off the Chapstick and studies it closely. Four officials going through it and suddenly hot steel fingers make a fist in his stomach: in the middle of the miscellanea, a small aluminum dime imprinted with "Southern Michigan State Prison Inmate Store." Big as a manhole cover. Nonchalantly reach out and pick it up, directly into the mouth . . . can't swallow, mouth too dry, but it doesn't matter. Nobody notices. Four uniformed officials inspecting every detail of the handful of articles in front of them, and none notices him reach into the pile, remove something and put it into his mouth. He smiles . . . this is a sign. I will walk away from this. Finally the female in the fancy uniform hands over a voucher for cab fare back to the U.S. side. Deported As An Undesirable Alien. Close call. On the American side, a man in a suit flashes a badge and escorts him into another office with three more officials. Duffel bag dumped out, the same questions in rapid fire. Going through the clothes. Please do not grasp the significance of the number stamped in most of them. Finally, get out of here and don't try that shit again. Yessir, sorry to have been a bother. Is there somewhere nearby a guy can get a drink? Beat it. Yessir . . .

Back to Greyhound for refund. Ticket lady laughs . . . knew they would send you back. Thanks for telling me. Not my job to tell you where you can't go; my job's to sell tickets. Right, sell me one for Chicago.

Windy City, three hours later: long-shot call to biker dude known from years past. Actually make contact, he remembers favor done long ago and far away. Stay still, be down to get you. Nothing conspicuous about a dozen Hell's Angels roaring through the terminal. Hey man, hop on. Two hours later, O'Hare International Airport, with a few hundred bucks—thanx, man—and an Illinois driver's license. Some guy fifteen years older, fifty pounds heavier and bald. But picture identification. "One way to Toronto, please." This time, piece of cake. Quick glance at license, enjoy your visit. God save the Queen.

Toronto is good. Pretty, no pollution, nice people. Lotsa trees, parks everywhere. Museums. Cozy place to live and library card first day. Job and identification next day. Military out of the question for a dozen reasons. Oh well.

Four months later: Oops, gotta go. Leaving town with less than arrived with. Stroll across bridge at Niagara Falls, hitchhike to Texas.

Changes in latitude, changes in attitude . . .

SECTION 3:
A CAT NAMED JIMMY BUFFET

THE LAID-BACK AND THE WASTED

A few years back, I dropped out of the human race and moved out into the sticks. I hunted furs for a living and raised ducks for amusement. For company, I had a cat with an I.Q. somewhere right up there with eggshells. It was an uncomplicated life and I had few complaints.

City living is much more stressful than a guy like me needs. It got to the point I was cussing people in traffic, trying to rush people in the grocery store checkout line, generally acting just like people that I intensely dislike. I was going around with my shoulders all scrunched up in knots and becoming more misanthropic every day. The job, too many people, pollution, too many people. And of course, just too damn many people. Finally I confronted myself with this philosophical question: Do I need this? Answer: No, I do not.

One day Jimmy Buffet, my little Siamese buddy, and I were exploring the woods near our place and found a really neat pond. We soon discovered that this was a favorite hangout for wild ducks and geese, as well as a multitude of other woodland creatures. There were kazillions of eggs around, a large percentage of which had already fallen victim to coyotes and other egg-sucking varmints—most notably coons. We rushed into town and bought one of those little incubators they sell at the feed store and set up shop. We could set forty eggs at a time and that is what we started with. First guy out of his shell was a little goose. He had a pretty rough time of it there for his first week or so and spent most of the time sitting in my hand, snuggled up against me. It was the damnedest thing: that silly bird fixated on me and took to following me around all over the place.

Country living agreed with me. There is little stress, and any number of cathartic ways to deal with what little does come along. For example, not long after I moved, I was over in Cherokee and saw this tricked-out '55 Chevy parked in front of the post office (which is also a grocery store, gas station, and community gossip center). This was a show-quality vehicle, worth more money than everything I owned put together. There were a couple guys of the Not-From-Around-These-Parts variety sitting in it, exuding all kinds of Bad Attitude. They seemed offended that I was giving their wheels such scrutiny. I said, "Nice car." (I am a man of few words.) They just sat there and nailed me with this badass stare meant to be intimidating. (Actually, it reminded me of junior high.) I blew it off and headed for the ranch. On the way home, though, it sort of crept up on me. Just who the hell did they think they were, anyway? I slowed down a couple times and started to turn around and go back. Soon as I got home, I grabbed a maul and attacked a big pile of firewood that needed to be split. By the time I finished, all the anger, stress and tension had disappeared, replaced by the satisfaction that comes with the completion of honest physical labor. If I still lived in that third floor walk-up, surrounded by asphalt, where would I have channeled all that negative energy? I don't know, but it wouldn't have been pretty.

I could carry on all day on the things I love about living in the country, but let me just mention one thing most people take for granted: trees. I love trees. In a group of them, even in a forest, I see every one of them individually. To me, a tree is just a big old wooden flower. They are so majestic. I can generate some real hostility toward people who abuse trees. Like, I cringe when I see someone pound nails into them. I knew some people whose home was surrounded by the most beautiful old red maples there ever were. They had them all reduced to kindling because they interfered with their satellite dish reception. I am still sick about that. I had a favorite tree out there about half way between my place and town. This was a big old black walnut, about twenty-five feet off the road.

I lived in great fear for this beauty. Black walnut mills out into some exquisite lumber and is highly prized by cabinet makers and such people. A tree of this size could be worth several thousand dollars. There are folks who will come in the night with a chainsaw and steal a tree like this right out of your yard. Can you believe that?

My ducks were my little buddies. Duck eggs are a little tricky in an incubator; they tend to get brittle and harder than they would under natural circumstances. In the wild, these eggs are subject to constant moisture, which softens them and makes it easier for the little dudes to break out. Quite a few of mine I ended up having to peel out of their shells and hand feed for the first few days. There was a bond there. Ducklings like these were selling for three dollars a pop downtown. Mine sold for whatever, most of them by the way of barter. I took laying hens, fish hooks, goat milk, fresh honey, pickled peppers, jalapeno jelly, and, basically, just whatever. I wasn't in it for the money. I only let them go because I ended up with hundreds of them little rascals and couldn't bring myself to eat them. The goose, Mr. Peepers, stayed with me, though. He was part of the family.

I kind of got a kick out of that goofy bird following me around all the time and started taking him along with me when I went into town. In Texas, it's pretty much mandatory to have a dog in your pickup at all times; either in the cab, head hanging out the window, tongue flapping in the wind, or in the back end—that part is optional. I didn't have a dog. I had a goose. The old boys had a problem with that. I would pull up to the curb, me and my goose would hop out, and he would follow me around as I did my errands. People used to shake their heads and say, "There's something wrong with that boy."

Mr. Peepers was with me the second time I saw those guys in the Chevy. They were sitting there, so cool, without moving, but following me with their eyes as I walked along the sidewalk. When I was right in front of them, I turned and gave them my best politician smile, and said, "Hey fellas, nice car!" There was no visible reaction, but I know they were doubly insulted when Peepers, bringing up the rear, turned and hissed at them.

What I usually did in town was drop a handful of grain outside the door before I went into the post office or wherever. Peepers would be content to nibble away on that until I came out for him. Sometimes it took longer than expected, and he would just be sitting there waiting for me. This particular day, I heard him squawking and flapping around out there, and I ran out to find him running in circles, bumping into things, stumbling over rocks, and generally freaking out. There was some slimy rust-colored crud all over his head and dripping off his beak. It took a few minutes to realize that someone had sploshed a big old glob of chewing tobacco juice right in his little face. I carried him over and held his head under a faucet near the gas pumps. I looked around for the culprit, but there was no one in sight. That was probably a good thing. There could have been some violence.

I was having a real problem that winter with coons. They kept sneaking in and killing my ducks. It was just ridiculous the extremes I went to trying to keep them out. They were unstoppable. I couldn't set traps because I didn't want to catch my cats. It was about this time I learned about a place over in Cherokee that bought coon skins for twenty bucks apiece. That's all I needed to know. Those coons were in trouble after that. The sport of killing my ducks was replaced by a new game called "Dodge the Flashlight Beam."

So one day coming out of Cherokee, I was feeling chipper from having sold a big pile of pelts when that cherry '55 Chevy flew by me at about 100 mph. The clown on the passenger side spit a big mouthful of tobacco juice just in time for it splatter across my windshield. They both got an enormous laugh out of that. What had started as a pretty decent day was quickly turning into one of those numbers that leads to a good supply of firewood. I was contemplating that when the Chevy, now a good half mile ahead of me, blew a tire. The car did an immediate sharp turn to the right and into the ditch on that side of the road. The ditch was configured in such a way, though, that it actually acted as a launching ramp. No telling how far that baby would have flown if someone hadn't planted that black walnut tree right there many years ago.

By the time I got there, several cars had pulled over. Me and this high school kid walked over to inspect the damage. The Chevy was totaled. The front end was severely U'ed from where it had kissed the tree. There were two bloody spiderwebs on the windshield. The velocity of the impact was great enough that the car actually bounced back about ten feet after its initial contact with the tree. A very large patch of bark was torn off the tree and the wood underneath had been seriously assaulted. The kid next to me had never seen anything like this before. The blood drained from his face and his knees appeared to be a little rubbery. In a sort of breathless whisper he said, "Shouldn't we do something?"

I said, "There really isn't anything we can do. Something like this, you just have to let nature take its course. She'll probably drop her leaves and go dormant early this year and try to heal her wounds from within. We won't have any way of knowing how she'll come out of this until next spring, but I'm guessing she'll be okay. These old walnuts are pretty tough."

I started walking back to my truck. The kid caught up with me and said, "But what about that?" indicating the wrecked Chevy.

"That," I shrugged, "*was* a nice car."

A Cat Named Jimmy Buffet

When I moved out into the country, I had one badly abused mobile home, a mentally retarded Siamese cat, and one thousand back issues of *Mother Earth News*. I was at a place in my life where I just did not want to be around people. Maybe you have to be a Cat Person to appreciate just how much company a cat can be; I didn't have much to do with the human race there for a while, but I was never lonely. This guy's name was Jimmy Buffet. Living together in that kind of seclusion, we got to know one another pretty well. It was actually a bit overwhelming how much this little creature trusted and depended on me. He was so skittish, he wouldn't even come into the house when someone else was there, but he seemed to enjoy being with me. I felt like we communicated pretty well. After a while we bought an incubator and hatched out a wild goose egg. That goofy bird fixated on me and followed me all over the place. It was hysterical. We were three serious misfits.

I used to think I would never have a Siamese cat, just because they are so popular. Everybody has one. I like those offbeat breeds like Rexes and those ones that have just skin but no hair at all. I once had a Maine coon cat named Mr. Big who weighed in at twenty-four pounds. His nickname was "Large" and he was *so cool*; his every move and pose was an expression of the ultimate feline. Jimmy Buffet was my little buddy, though, and the neatest cat I ever knew. I miss that little joker. He stuck with me when nobody else in the world was interested.

One great benefit of country living is free food. I moved out in the sticks a strict vegetarian, had been for years. One of my neighbors finally talked me into trying a taste of this smoked sausage he made out of venison and wild pig. (Want to be looked at like you're from Mars? Go out into the heart of Texas cattle country and say right out loud that you don't eat meat.) Anyway, this was one of those life-changing experiences. That stuff was delicious. And it was free. Poor as I was, I suddenly felt stupid for not eating dead animals. Next day I went to the pawn shop and bought a rifle.

A month or so before I moved, there was an ad in the Austin paper that just said "CATS," with an address that happened to be in the neighborhood. (This was long before the Broadway production.) Something compelled me to stop over and check it out. The place was a nightmare. This enormous blob of a woman had a houseful of the scrawniest, sickliest, most pitiful felines I have ever seen. They were absolutely everywhere around the house, which reeked in a way that made my eyes water. A couple dead fish on the floor were being gnawed by some truly wretched looking creatures.

As I was backing toward the door, a tiny Siamese caught my attention. He was sitting on a bookshelf—raggedy, flea-infested, and sick as a dirty yellow dog—and had the brightest blue eyes in all creation. His eyes were the color of bluebonnets (which for the benefit of youse Yankees is the state flower of Texas). I asked Miss Piggy how much for him and she told me forty bucks. I held out an Abe Lincoln and said, "Close enough?" It instantly disappeared, and I picked this little guy up and got him out of there as fast as I could. In a tiny, utterly weary little voice he said, "Peep." I said, "You're welcome."

Folks out in the Hill Country say there are two types of people when it comes to "buzztails" (rattlesnakes): either you got sense enough to leave 'em alone or you are some kind of damn fool. There is no in-between. I couldn't leave them suckers alone. I never passed a flat rock or old log without flipping it over, hoping to find one. This part of the world tends to be very clannish and xenophobic. You can be there for three generations and the natives will still say, "They ain't *from* heya." I was officially recognized as a Good Ole Boy by the locals the day I went "den wallowing" with some of the neighborhood maniacs. That meant little to me—I'm not exactly a social butterfly—but anyone moving out there who wants to be accepted can take a lesson. As soon as I heard about this activity, I could hardly contain myself until a day finally came along that was weather permitting.

One of my favorite albums back in those days was Jimmy Buffet's *Changes in Latitude, Changes in Attitude*. My little kitten and I were listening to this shortly after he escaped Blob Woman From Hell when I realized he really liked it, too. I used to listen to music all the time back then and normally he didn't seem to notice, but he always seemed to react to this L.P. I asked him if he liked Jimmy Buffet and he said, "Ow," which I interpreted to mean, "Jimmy Buffet! That's my name, too!" I guess you had to know him the way I did. Jimmy Buffet—or sometimes "J.B.," sometimes "Buffet," never "Jimmy"—spent those first few weeks curled up in the palm of my hand snuggled against my stomach. This was one tiny cat. Siameses are famous for their intelligence, but I gotta tell you, Buffet wasn't all that swift. In fact, he was about the dumbest feline I ever knew. He was also clumsy. At first I thought it was because he had one crossed eye, but that straightened out as he got older, and he still fell off the edge of things he was walking on and was just pitiful as a tree climber. I'll say this for the little dude, though: he wasn't smart, but he was sure good looking. He had chocolate points on his ears and tail, four perfect socks and a really neat mask around his eyes. Naturally, I'm biased, but I honestly believe he was as fine looking a Siamese as any I've seen at cat shows.

I got a snake story that'll knock your socks off. This one even gives me the creeps. Me and this ole boy I met out at the den wallow were out checking fish traps one night (at night because fish traps of this nature do not fall comfortably within the definition of "strictly legal"). We were walking upstream emptying fish into mesh bags that were about six feet long, which floated along behind us. After about forty-five minutes, Leroy glanced over his shoulder and did this sharp intake of air that so effectively expresses sudden terror. I looked back and my flashlight beam lit up about one hundred million pair of beady little red eyes and slithering black tails, which accounted for pretty much every cottonmouth snake in the known world. They were *right there*. Cottonmouths—also known as water moccasins—eat fish. And yes, these snakes do have fangs like sabre tooth tigers, and yes, they will kill you. The water was roiling from the masses of writhing black serpents slithering around all over each other, over and around those mesh bags full of yummy things to eat. It was a scene straight out of a horror movie, all the more horrifying for being silent.

We both had the presence of mind to let go of the bags and keep on walking. The area we were in had steep banks on either side, heavily overgrown with mesquite and shrubs. All we could do was keep on walking straight ahead, looking for a place to get out of the river. About twenty-five feet from where we let the snakes have our fish, we looked back. The water was thrashing and foaming, creating enough turbulence to make waves that reached us that far away. It was the best part of an hour before we were able to get out of the water; I don't mind telling you, that whole thing still creeps me out. I aged about ten years right there.

It didn't take me long to learn that the most effective way to drop a carcass of venison is to do so at night. The technique is to tape a flashlight onto the rifle barrel and sort of sweep the beam back and forth as you walk along. When the light hits the deer's eyes, they light up like little round lightbulbs. Smaller creatures, like coon, their eyes light up red. This was in country where cattle free-range, so it was important to learn the difference between cow eyes and deer eyes. They still hang cattle rustlers out there.

Since it came up, I want to tell you a thing or two about raccoons. Everybody thinks those wretched creatures are just so freaking cute. Let me tell you something: them suckers are more vile than sewer rats. The thing about them is that they are so smart, and they have actual hands, so it is nigh onto impossible to keep them out of anything they want in to. The bottom line on coons is that they are evil. They kill little animals just for the sheer joy of it. They are really vicious. Where the coons of Llano county went wrong was making a sport of killing my ducks in a season that a good coon skin was worth twenty bucks. Bad time to make me hate you if you're a coon. I was out coon hunting pretty much every night that winter. Those pelts were covering most of my expenses.

It came time to make that big decision about Buffet's progeny. Cats are driven by their hormones more than any other creature. That's why toms usually do not live long and prosper. It was a really tough decision, but finally I took J.B. in for The Operation. I mean, life was hard enough already for the little guy. Did he need girl problems, too? He got so tired of me apologizing, he moved out into the woods for about a week until I got over it.

I only mention that by way of telling you something else about Buffet. Six months or so after that, Julie Margaret McIntyre came to live with us. "Julie" for this coffee house singer in San Antonio I was crazy about—who was crazy about another singer named Mary Beth, but that's another story—"Margaret" for the princess (no kidding) and "McIntyre" for Reba. She was also Siamese. We all decided that Jewels was so pretty she should go ahead and have a litter of kittens. When she came into season, Buffet was freaking out. Jewels was walking around bawling and squalling and hollering and poor Buffet just didn't know what to make of it. He was very upset, but he hung out. He stayed there with her the whole time. All he knew was that the girl was suffering, and he was there for her. He wasn't too bright, but his little heart was in the right place.

The worst thing that happened in Jimmy Buffet's young life was, one night he was out playing in the woods and got bit by a rattlesnake. He came running in and woke me up, crying and jumping around. He was bleeding from two little punctures in his right arm. Julie and I ran him into town and got Doc out of bed. Buffet pulled through but he was never quite the same after that. There was nerve damage and his little paw drew up all stumpy-looking, and—what he could stand less than anything—there was brain damage, which is common in snake bite. Poor little Jimmy Buffet came out of that experience dumber than ever. For months after that, once in a while he would stop and shake his paw and lick it and cry. He would turn those baby blues in my direction all full of "Help me." I'm telling you, it would tear the heart out of Hitler.

Julie had her litter and it was a real circus around there for a while. Never did know who the dad was, but that's the thing about cats: we had no neighbors for miles in any direction, but somehow two unrelated domestic cats managed to find one another. Eventually all of them, Mom included, found new homes and it was back to just me and Buffet. He liked it better that way and I felt a little guilty having the others around. The little ones drove him crazy and Julie always wanted to hang out with him, knowing full well that he was a loner. It wasn't fair to complicate his life like that.

There is a place up in the rocks outside of Cherokee that is just perfect for den wallowing. This is done on a cold day when the snakes are sluggish. There is a roughly V-shaped crevasse in the rocks about ten feet deep, just wide enough for some damn fool to lay on his back on the bottom. It's a tight fit. The way you play this game is to lay flat on your back down there, which puts the opening of the snake den about six inches over your face. Rattlesnakes react to gasoline; it burns them. So, the trick is, you take one of these pump-up sprayers, like you use on garden pests, and fill it up with gasoline. Attach a length of copper tubing to the nozzle so that it extends into the den, *behind* the mass of snakes, and spray the gas in. The only way for them to escape is through the tunnel you are guarding the entrance of with your face. As soon as one of those rascals sticks his head out, you grab him around the throat, haul him out and hand him up so the guys up there can take him with the tongs. There will be another immediately behind the first, so it gets a bit dicey. By this time, the snakes have an attitude and really, *really* want to bite somebody. In the case in point, that would be me. After a few minutes of this, I felt like I'd had enough, but that's the catch. You can't just quit. There is no such thing as getting up to leave before the last buzztail is out of the den. At that point, a good stiff shot of Jose Cuervo is in order.

If you handle the whole den without getting bit, you win. If you do get bit, you're judged on how cool you are about it because, hey, snakebit or not, there's no coming out of there before the last snake has left home. Unless you want to get bit again, in which case you lose. Think about the kind of people who would call this a good time and it won't be hard to imagine some ole boy waiting until the guy down there is struggling to not lose it, dragging a six foot long, hissing, vibrating rattlesnake across his face, fangs dripping venom in his eyes, then reaching down there and poking him in the ankle with a sharp stick. This is a real knee-slapper. No matter how heartfelt your "That ain't funny, man!", when it's your turn to do it to the next guy, it really is amusing. Life is funny like that.

97

Some rattlesnake trivia: them suckers stink. You can smell a snake den a long way off. It's hard to get that smell off your hands. When you lay on your back and drag a couple hundred of them across yourself, fangs dripping venom—which has its own reek—by the end of the day, you like to never get that smell off you. It makes for a memorable experience, though.

Later on that night, I went out hunting and walked for miles. It was spitting rain off and on, much colder than normal, and a good night to have stayed home. Not one deer or fur-bearing varmint in sight. After about five hours I was heading back to the ranch and picked up a couple little red lights about a hundred feet from my property line. It was an easy shot. When I ran up to collect my prize, I was disappointed to see it was just a big old jackrabbit. Strange markings, though. It had a sort of mask, and socks, and the ears were all wrong. It also had a long, chocolate point tail. It took a minute to realize it wasn't a jack at all.

My goose friend grew up to be mean and aggressive like every other dumbass goose I ever knew. He got one stern warning, but the second time he bit me, he was reduced to Thanksgiving dinner for some folks I knew who had nine kids and not much else. They said he was delicious.

I buried Jimmy Buffet in a pretty spot near where he used to hang out a lot and planted bluebonnets all around for him. Buffet always liked bluebonnets. Rest in peace, little buddy.

I don't listen to those albums anymore.

SECTION 4:
NONE OF THE ABOVE

COWBOYS AND INJURIES

C owboys are generally regarded as riff-raff. It's not hard to under-stand why. There has to be something wrong with anyone who will work that hard for less than minimum wage, who is subject to come up missing without notice and is more than likely drinking on the job. Cowboys drift from ranch to ranch, building up a stake and then pressing on. During the season, someone with the necessary skills can sign on pretty much anywhere, toss his gear in the bunkhouse and go to work. It's a rough way to make a living, but it is flexible. As an English-speaking Anglo knowledgeable in the ways of a working ranch and will-ing to work like a rented slave, I was considered a catch.

The last season I cowboyed, I was on with Grey Ranch, Inc., an enor-mous Central Texas spread. The Greys had twenty-five thousand acres of peanuts under irrigation—we're talking a couple million bucks right there—and also ran about the same acreage in beef. That's not to mention the horses, pecan orchards, and the rest of it. At that time they were grad-ually going the way of many others: building up a goat herd with an eye toward replacing the entire cattle operation with dairy goats. There are good reasons for doing so. Some of the old hands thought it was demean-ing to be a "goat roper" rather than a bona fide cowboy, but to me it was a no-brainer: would I rather be rounding up a passel of sixty-five pound goats or a bunch of six hundred pound beefs? There are no horror stories being told around campfires about entire crews of goat ropers trampled to death by a herd of unruly dairy goats.

Grey Ranch was owned and operated by The Boss. An old cowhand himself, The Boss was all you could expect of a man in his position—he was hard, ornery, profane and demanding, but a fair and decent guy for all that. The personage most feared at Grey Ranch was The Missus. The Missus kept her distance from the hired help as a rule, but on those occasions when she made an appearance, heads rolled. It was never a happy omen to look up and see her coming. One of the Mexicans I worked with described her as "the meanest white woman I ever knew." No one disputed that.

The Boss and The Missus lived in The Big House, which was well-removed from everything else on the property. It was understood there was no reason to approach The Big House of one's own volition. I was never tempted. One afternoon, however, a particularly spunky young goat made a mad dash for freedom through a cracked gate. Being on horseback at the time, I set out in pursuit. We ended up near the back porch of The Big House by the time I had a lasso around his neck. At that point, I looked down at the shortest cowpoke I had ever seen on a working Texas cattle ranch. He stood about four foot five, sported a fancy double holster rig with matching pearl handled six shooters, a patent leather vest and suede cowboy boots. Curly red hair escaped around the edges of his black felt cowboy hat. Eyeing me suspiciously, he carefully drew iron and announced, "I'll blow your kneecap off." To which I responded, "I'll gouge your eyeballs out and squish 'em like rotten grapes." His face lit up with delight. "I'll stomp a Mexican mud hole right in the middle of your back," he spat back immediately. Before I could respond to that, The Missus burst through the door, grabbed the little gunslinger by the wrist and slammed the door behind them, all in one motion. My charge and I returned to the corral.

About a week later, I was busy chasing a rattlesnake across the lawn with a macheté and, from about a hundred feet away, heard an upstairs window in The Big House creak open. An eager little voice hollered at me, "I'll rip your lungs out and play 'em like a bagpipe!" I called back, "I'll twist your big toes off and stuff 'em up your nostrils!" "I'll tear . . ."

he began, but the window suddenly slammed shut in a manner that told me once again that The Missus was not amused.

It went on like that throughout the summer. I never knew the kid's name or actually saw much of him. For all I knew, he didn't leave the house or play with other kids. It occurred to me later that he must have spent an inordinate amount of time looking out the window, because any time I was within shouting distance, the wind would carry that reedy little voice issuing some dire threat of bodily atrocity. If the situation didn't allow for a proper response on my part, I would just put on my fiercest scowl and shake my fist in that direction. It always felt like a window or door slammed shut somewhere in the house when I did.

Life was hectic in those days. If the peanut crop failed, The Boss would be in the red for something similar to the national debt. A good harvest was a joyous occasion for all. Most people just casually munch on peanuts without the foggiest what it took to put those little goobers into their sweaty hands. You'd be amazed. Plus, while all that was going on, there were hundreds of thousands of dollars in beef on the hoof out there. The busiest times for both operations culminated at approximately the same time. Cowboys are worked with less consideration than pack mules. The one good thing about it was job security. Nobody has ever been fired at the peak of the season.

It was during this time that I was in one of the outbuildings adjusting the hydraulics on a peanut-picking machine when my little buddy sashayed on in with a Louisville Slugger over his shoulder to announce, "I'll knock your teeth so far down your throat, you'll have to drop your britches to floss." I told him I would hang him up by his heels and drive that bat through one ear and out the other with a twelve pound sledge hammer. "I'll pull your intestines out through your left ear and wrap 'em around your neck and hang you from a live oak tree," he countered. Before he got all that out, The Missus came stomping across the lawn with a seriously no-nonsense look on her face. Did that woman have satellite dishes for ears? My little friend was once again snatched up by the wrist and drug off behind a slammed door.

Less than an hour later, The Boss and I were conferring over the best course of action to take with a lame colt when his general foreman arrived to announce that The Missus had declared me *persona non grata* and if I was not off the property within ten minutes, she'd have the sheriff find out why. The Boss raised his eyebrows and looked at me for an explanation. "Women," I said and shrugged.

"Yeah," The Boss agreed and scratched his neck. The three of us stood there in silence waiting for The Boss to either veto it or make it official. After a few moments of serious contemplation he looked up and said, "This ain't right, and it's not fair to you. You're a damn good hand and we need you right now." He paused for a long moment and then continued, "On the other hand, The Missus can be a natural bitch to live with when she don't get her way, and cowboys are a dime a dozen. I'm sorry, son. I really am." I shrugged again and asked for my hours. We figured it up and he paid me cash out of his pocket. Cowboys don't waste a lot of verbiage on questions whose answers don't matter or on stating the obvious. When it is understood that "this is just the way it is," there's nothing left to say. You suck it up and push on.

I returned to the bunkhouse and tossed my gear in the back of my truck and, instead of driving straight down to the county road, took the long way out, through the blueberry thicket, past the stables, and onto the drive that went back around by The Big House. My little buddy came running out and hollered, "I'll twist your head around with a monkey wrench so you'll have to walk backwards to see where you're going." I told him, "I'll crank your nose upside down so you'll drown the next time it rains." The Missus was standing on the porch a few feet away watching but evoked no expression and did not interfere.

"I'll pull your tongue out by the roots and staple it to your forehead," he shouted in a very unsteady voice. I let the truck idle toward the gate while my friend ran along beside. We exchanged a few more threats and I braked at the road. "Well, you take care of yourself, little partner." His teary eyes appeared enormous behind the thick lenses. "You too, Cowboy," he said in a quivery little voice. This was the only exchange we ever had that didn't involve mutilation, and the longest time we had ever spent in one another's company. He suddenly burst out crying and ran back to the house. This time the door did not slam when The Missus took him inside.

THE HEADLINE

The headline in our local slander sheet this morning reads "Biker Goes on Murder Rampage." Stuff like that makes me sick. Newspapers have so much power, people just don't realize. Shame on you if you happen to be poor, or the wrong color, or of a lifestyle some editor doesn't approve of. The biker's name is Aleksandr Josiah Demanzimjk. A mouthful, isn't it? I am quite possibly the only person you'll meet who can pronounce it correctly. For good reason—it's my name, too; that nasty old biker is my brother. I want to tell you, as Paul Harvey would say, The Rest of the Story.

First of all, don't let that name throw you. My family has been here long enough to have sacrificed sons to every bloody conflict since the War of Northern Aggression. When he started school, my brother was automatically dubbed Alphabet Soup, which evolved into Alphie. He hated that name, so, of course, that's what kids just had to call him. The summer between sixth and seventh grade, though, he grew about a foot and a half and put on something like two hundred pounds. When school started in the fall, they didn't call him Alphie anymore. Since that time he's been known as Soup.

Soup is the kind of guy, he walks down the street—hair to his waist, bandana around his head, bike club colors, hobnail boots—people step out of his way. It's funny, because in reality, the guy is a teddy bear. Oh, don't get me wrong: the man can be a beast. What I'm saying is, he's not looking for trouble. Leave him alone and he hardly ever bites; do him right and you've got a friend for life.

Me and Soup, we been scooter tramps all our lives. We was born to it. To look at us, you wouldn't think we knew anything about "family values" and all that fancy stuff. (I'm about as pretty as my brother although not nearly as big.) The fact is, we come from a very close family: that's the thing I wanted to tell you about. Our dad died when we was just kids, and it was up to me and Soup and Moms. Just a couple months after that, B.B.—for Baby Bro—was born. Between having had a tough life in general, losing her husband, and having one hell of a time carrying B.B. and bringing him into the world, Moms was just real tired, you know? Soup automatically took over as man of the house. That dude never had a childhood. He assigned me chores (like, I had to walk along the railroad tracks and pick up the coal that fell off the coal cars for our stove), and all kinds of stuff that normal kids didn't have to do, but he let me be a kid at the same time. He made Moms lay down as soon as she came home and waited on her hand and foot. Moms was so worn out, though, and she really just wanted to go On Home, you understand. And one night, she went to bed and did just that.

That was rough, but when you are dirt-poor white trash, grief is a luxury you don't wallow in. You bury your head and get on with it. Life goes on, and there were other matters demanding attention.

Like B.B. That little guy was just born under a bad sign. As a baby he couldn't keep anything in his stomach. He cried for hours on end. The whole house smelled like baby puke and we were all exhausted from lack of sleep. Doctors couldn't offer anything beyond the idea that he was high-strung and would grow out of it. Eventually he did, but that was when his nightmares began. It got to where if we passed the night without being awakened by blood-chilling screams, Soup would go and check on him to see what was wrong. Something was terrorizing that kid, and it dogged him for years.

Nothing was easy, but we got by. Soup never really went to school after sixth grade, and I dropped out in junior high. Between us, we kept the place going. It became apparent that Moms knew she wasn't in it for the long haul; it turned out that we had been taught a lot of important lessons about how to scratch our daily bread out of a little piece-of-nothing farm, and some important survival skills that made all the difference. We appreciated her more and more as time went on.

When other kids our age were getting excited about their first prom, me and Soup were certified members of an outlaw motorcycle club. We kept B.B. in school, checked his homework, and made every attempt to see that he was ready for whatever opportunities might come his way. If you know how kids are, you can imagine how they treated him at school, though. A scrawny, off-beat kid from a scooter trash family, living out in the sticks. He didn't have any friends, had no interest in sports, and just really didn't seem to have any real purpose in life. Soup fretted over it. He was the little dude's mother and father, his best friend and guardian angel. There was a bond between them I never had with anyone.

One day Soup brought home this basket-case Honda 160. Not a big bike, but not a toy, either. It was in a million pieces. Soup told B.B. this would be his first wheel. "When you are on the highway on a scooter, you're trusting your life to it," Soup explained solemnly. "Do you want to be flying along on a machine put together by some zit-faced kid or some damn foreigner?" B.B. shook his head. "Of course you don't," Soup continued. "What you want to do is build your own sled from the ground up. You want to know every nut and bolt, every ding and scratch, like it is a part of yourself, and you don't ever want anybody else's wrench to touch it. Do you?" B.B. shook his head. "Here's your owner's manual, and here's your tool kit. Have at it; don't be afraid to ask questions." Great idea, Soup, and I salute you for the effort, but this kid has never expressed an interest in anything. Building a scooter from a pile of parts is a pretty big job.

I've been wrong before. The kid sat down, studied the manual, and went to work. It was slow, frustrating, tedious, and could not have been much fun. Soup had to go out there about midnight and make him blow it off until the next day. After that, you never saw the kid without a socket wrench or his face in some kind of motorcycle magazine. He had that machine up and running in just a couple of weeks. By all rights, that should have been a job that lasted all summer. Pretty soon, he was buzzing around the place like a maniac. I never saw a little dude so content. He still didn't smile or say much of anything or show what you might go so far as to term excitement, but he had found something that interested him and seemed to make him happy, and that was cool. We only had a couple of acres out there, and Soup wouldn't let him ride on the road until he had a license. Soup was strict with the kid; he wouldn't let him do anything illegal.

One day, Soup piled the Honda into the back of his truck and we all went out to the east pits, which is a huge complex of gravel pits, about five miles square, out east of town. All the pits are full of water; some are pretty much bottomless and connected by tunnels that create undertows and all kinds of weird things. You can throw something in one of them and have it show up the next day in another pit a mile away. Several high school kids have made it their business to drown out there in the last few years, so it's closed to swimming now. There are some really great little trails running through there, though, and in the winter, snowmobilers are out by the hundreds. Anyway, we unloaded the iron steed and told the kid to go for it. He didn't have to be told twice. He flew around this mountain of gravel and that was the last we saw of him for the rest of the day. How can I say this? The roar of the engine even sounded happy. We didn't mind hanging around all day waiting on him, the way he was digging it. He was getting to know his wheel, learning its power, its limitations. We heard him stop and adjust his carbs and experiment with different settings. We heard him dump it a few times, and that was cool, too. You gotta pay your dues. Finally, right around sundown, we heard him run out of gas and waited for him to push it back to the truck. We coulda went and picked him up, but Soup said that's part of being a biker, too— sometimes you gotta push that sucker.

When the kid came around the corner of that mountain, I gotta tell you, something caught in my throat and I had to turn away. I thought Soup was going to start blubbering. There are no words for the transformation that took place that day out there at the pits. That scrawny, half-alive kid we sent off on that little Honda evaporated sometime during the afternoon. The little dude who returned was absolutely glowing. I mean, the kid was lit up. You know how an ugly caterpillar turns into a beautiful monarch butterfly? You ever see the dried up little seeds that produce the most exquisite flowers in the world? Leonardo turned globs of paint into works the world has been in awe of for the past couple hundred years. Forget about that. The change that took place out there that day was too astounding for words. The kid had finally come around. For the first time in his life, he was happy. He had found his niche, and I'm telling you, I don't think Soup or I had ever been quite so happy, either.

We stopped off at the bar where the club hangs out and ordered up some brewskis to celebrate. I really loved those guys that night. They immediately dug what was happening and they gave the kid the floor. Most of them had known him since he was a tyke, and they knew his history. No one had ever heard him put more than a couple of words back to back, and this in a mumble while staring at his toes. Now he was alive, talking to a bunch of bikers who had been on wheels longer than he'd been breathing, straining to find words to express the exhilaration, the wind in his face, the power of the throttle, the proper carb settings, the sheer joy of being on a motorcycle and having the wind whip his hair. They gave him their full attention and let him get it all said, and not all patronizing like, either, but in a respectful way. I mean, they dug what was happening and they were happy for the little guy. Old Barney even pretended not to notice when Soup gave the kid his first beer. One of the chicks introduced him to her little sister, and they hit it off just like that. I overheard him telling her that he didn't go for all the bells and whistles and shiny objects, just your basic motorcycle built to perform well and look good. Talk that talk, little bro.

After that day at the pits, everything was different. We would all sit around the house kicking it around like brothers do. Soup would let the kid have a beer or two; we suddenly had a little brother we had never known before. He was a real all right kind of guy, too. I mean, this was someone I was proud to call my brother. I gotta tell you, my respect for Soup just skyrocketed. (Do you think one of those two hundred bucks an hour shrinks could have brought the kid around like that?) It was neat. We had never been so much a family before. As often as possible, we'd haul the kid and his machine out to the pits and come back to pick him up at sundown. Sometimes his little girlfriend would find her way out there and they would make a day of jamming around the trails and having a picnic on one of the dunes. Life was good.

I dunno. I still say those guys didn't mean no harm. Oh, they were wrong for sure, I'm just saying—you know how it is, you get to playing around and it gets a little rough, maybe somebody gets a bloody nose, but hey, no real harm done. Those guys couldn't possibly have known how it would tear B.B.'s heart out when they jumped on his bike and went jamming around on it, him running behind them, screaming like a maniac. They say when that big guy lost it on one of those sharp curves, B.B. didn't hesitate for a second to dive into the water after it. Cops finally found the bike and hauled it out, but still have found no trace of the kid.

When Soup left the house yesterday morning, he told me to leave him alone, and he meant it. I have never seen such a cold look in a man's eyes. Tell you the truth, he scared me. I wonder if those three guys in that bar across town had a chance to see that look when he strolled in with the twelve-gauge pump shotgun under his arm.

Rez Kid

t's really kinda weird. Sometimes when I try to tell about my childhood, people say, "That is so neat," and I want to tell them, "You're romanticizing it. It was squalid and gritty." Sometimes I can tell the same story and people will say, "Gee, it's so sad that kids have to grow up like that in this day and age," and I want to say, "You don't understand; we were wild and free and didn't even know we were poor." My friends all have kids now and sometimes I envy the way they get to grow up. But I know that if they could step into Mr. Peabody's Way Back Machine and spend what was a typical week in the life with us back then, it would be a story they'd tell endlessly and those vacations to Yellowstone and the Grand Canyon would pale by comparison.

I grew up on an Indian reservation in the southwestern United States. It was hot, dry, dusty, and not very pretty. Think of Appalachia without the mountain vistas, the Mississippi Delta without water, okay? Still today, my people live in house trailers, pre-fabricated homes, and rickety shacks with cardboard in the windows. Every yard is decorated with the rusting remains of old cars up on cinder blocks and every porch has an old refrigerator standing sentinel. Skinny, slat-sided dogs lope through the shimmering heat with rubber tongues hanging out the sides of lopsided smiles. Everyone is poor and has too many kids. The stuff the peo-

111

ple around here pour down their throats to get drunk would make a big city wino turn up his nose in disgust.

In spite of all that, I count myself lucky. I had two parents and neither of them were alcoholics. My dad and all four of his brothers enlisted in the Marine Corps right after Pearl Harbor and stayed on for a couple of hitches after the war. Uncle Sam ended up teaching them all some valuable trades, mostly related to construction. Between the five of them, they had every aspect of building something down pat. The G.I. Bill allowed them to all put up decent homes and start up a little construction business. It did all right for a decade or so but eventually petered out. There is just not enough money in these parts to keep such an enterprise going. They could have made big bucks elsewhere, but hey, crappy as it is, this little corner of paradise is Home Sweet Home.

We had a small ranch on the outskirts of what passed for "town." It seems strange to refer to it as "small." The parcel of land described on the deed was not large, but we were surrounded by thousands of acres of government land that was, for all intents and purposes, ours. We were pretty much self-sufficient in a way that is really cool if you live in a hippie commune. If you grow up that way, though, you salivate over the idea of a Big Mac, store candy or "real" ice cream out of a carton. I was enough of a red-blooded American kid to whine and moan about looking into a plate of turtle beans and venison again, knowing full well that there were those within shouting distance who would consider that a holiday meal.

There are some things about those days that I have grown to resent mightily, but I do have blessings to count. I am grateful that for all their sophistication—by local standards, you understand—my parents were traditional. We were raised to respect the Elders and revere our ancestors. We learned our native tongue, knew the significance of tribal songs and ceremonies, and were grateful for the wonders of nature. We were firmly rooted in the twentieth century; we just had enormous respect for our heritage and felt a solemn responsibility to keep it alive. I've had hair to my waist since I was eight; my left earlobe was pierced by my great-grandmother when I was three days old. All of that means something to me.

If you stand just about anywhere on this reservation and chuck a rock into the air, chances are it will come down and bonk someone who is my aunt, uncle or cousin or is married to one of the above. Just about every one of them are rodeo people. I have two cousins in wheelchairs and one in the cemetery behind cowboyin.' Some of my kinfolk ride the circuit, some just dabble in it, some raise bulls or train horses for the ring. One of my mom's brothers is a blacksmith and my grandpa makes custom saddles for show ponies. Kids I grew up with could name bulldoggers and bronc busters and quote their stats the way city kids do pro baseball players. My dad did some roping and riding back in the day and we raised a few horses, but for the most part, that rodeo bug pretty much passed over my family. I usta want to be a rodeo clown like my cousin Eddie and his brother in law—until I fell out of a treehouse when I was twelve. I'll let you in on a little secret about busted collar bones, purple and green bruises, and lacerations that require stitches: all that hurts. That's your life if you're a rodeo clown. At forty-five you're drawn up and crippled with arthritis and prematurely senile if you took too many hooves to the brain bucket. I'll pass.

Even so, when I was fourteen and got a chance to go out on the fall circuit, I jumped at it. Being on the road with a rodeo is like being with the circus; a lot of hard work setting up and tearing down the whole enchilada in a blur of one-horse towns. Across the Texas panhandle, Colorado, Wyoming and Montana in our case. My folks didn't want me to go, but didn't try to stop me. They knew I would come back changed, and I did. They knew I would be angry, and I was. They knew that I was a pretty happy kid there on the rez and would not be when I came back. They were right. In that time and place, though, fourteen was grown and time to get smacked in the face with a few realities.

When you grow up on a rez, you have a vague understanding that the world outside looks down on you. The government people who come around sometimes look at you like they have something nasty in their mouths, but are too polite to spit (but, gee whiz, who the hell cares? How do you take seriously anyone who wears a suit and tie in this climate? Get real!) When you get out into the world, though, and realize people are laughing at you, that there is an industry of toys and cartoons making a mockery of your grandparents, that schools teach kids that you are descended from savages who were not actual human beings, it all takes on a new perspective. When you realize that you have deliberately been deprived of an adequate education—well, I don't want to turn this into a prolonged bout of Ain't It A Shame. I'm just here to tell you a story.

Poor people work on cars. What else are we going to do—pay some mechanic twenty-five dollars an hour to work on a fifty dollar heap? People with money buy new cars with warranties; we buy junk and spend much of our waking lives under the hood, salvaging parts from those rusting skeletons in the yard. We wrap baling wire around connections that were never meant to be and just don't want to fit. We're always on the lookout for a bargain on a "parts car" or an old wreck that can be coaxed into squeezing out a few more miles. With this as a full-time pursuit, it is sometimes amazing what turns up. When I was a kid, we ended up in possession of an enormous old Cadillac. Even though it came our way for peanuts, it turned out to be a bad investment and was never driven on the street. One thing was its unquenchable thirst. In the end, it became a toy for my sisters and me. We treated it like a dune buggy and put hundreds of miles on the odometer tearing around the expanse of grassland surrounding our property. Some days it seemed like every kid on the rez, and most of the dogs, were piled into that ocean liner on wheels. It was so expensive to run, though, I started requiring everyone to bring along some gas to dump into the tank if they wanted to ride. I had kids showing up with soup cans full of gasoline siphoned from lawnmowers, beer bottles of diesel fuel and kerosene. It all went in. Either that old Caddy never knew the difference or it was a real forgiving old soul. It ran like a champ regardless of what we gave it to drink.

All of that was big fun, of course, but most of our ripping and running was on horseback. Horseflesh is bought, sold and traded in those parts even more obsessively than junk cars. Saddles and tack change hands all day long. My dad and uncles once snagged a bunch of wild mustangs and they became our breeding stock. Those suckers are mean in a big way, but they make great cow ponies. We never had a big operation, but we did have a nice little sideline going there for a while. My sisters and I all had our own animals from the time we were able to sit up straight.

The neatest thing we did as kids was camp out up in the hills on the edge of the reservation. It was a twenty mile trek on horseback to the small lake that was our destination. Roughly oval shaped, our lake had a surface area about the size of two football fields side by side. It was surrounded by woods, and reached only with great effort, which made it all the better. There was an old Chevy van up there which was the source of much speculation. It was completely surrounded by trees—not young saplings, but real, honest-to-God trees, in an area that is simply not accessible by motor vehicle. How on earth did that thing get there? Who knows? It was handy, though, because it gave us a place for long term storage. We had canvas tarps, tools, emergency rations, matches and a well-stocked first aid kit stashed there. First thing to do upon arrival was to pull out the tarps and throw up our teepees. No, this was not one of those "cultural pride" things. We built teepees for the same reason Plains Indians always have. They provide shelter from the elements and are quick and easy to put up and take down. We made a point of not bringing any food with us, outside of coffee, flour and salt. Our meals came out of the lake and surrounding woods.

A mile or so from our lake was a swamp that provided us with the turtle meat most of us had acquired a taste for. Catching snapping turtles is one of those delightful childhood activities that I look back on now and shudder. What you do is walk slowly through the swamp looking for the little bubbles that tell you one of those jokers is buried in the bottom mud right there. A snapping turtles' shell has bumpy ridges over his head and is smooth over the rear. The trick is, once you locate the turtle, you hold him down with one foot, and slide a stick around the outside of the shell. When you feel bumps, you know you are at the head end. It is important to keep all appendages away from that area. Having located the business end of this beast, you reach down and feel for the other end, grab the tail and lift that bad boy up out of the water, holding him well away from your body. When you see somebody around these parts who has air where a big chunk of hand should be or several missing fingers, chances are you are looking at a turtle hunter who has misjudged. It happens, and it's no joke.

The flip side of that, of course, is that it is great fun and snapping turtle is delicious. We always snagged a few to eat while we were there and usually took a couple home. This area was so secluded that the wildlife population was thriving. On a good trip we would bring down some venison or a wild pig. These outings lasted anywhere from a weekend to the best part of a month, depending on what had to be done at home. How many seven- or eight-year-old suburban kids could go off on an adventure like that? One time there was seven of us out there for three weeks and my sister Polly, at thirteen, was the oldest. Life was good in those days.

When we had turtles to take home, we would pen them up back at camp and take them home alive. On a trip we made when I was twelve, one of the really big ones escaped and got into the lake. This was terrifying. I mean, we swam nude up there (think about it). As luck would have it, this kid, Jamie, who was visiting from New Mexico, knew how to make turtle traps—knowledge which came from a boy scout handbook. How's that for cultural heritage? We wove a bunch of willow branches together and left the trap over night. I guess you know Jamie was viewed with some awe and enormous respect when we got up next morning and found a big old snapper in his trap. It was safe to go back into the water. Jamie came back later in the year and sold us on the idea of poisoning our lake. The fish we pulled out of it were small and boney. Jamie had read up on pond management and explained how we could kill off all the fish in there and then replace them with catfish fingerlings. There would be no trash fish gobbling up the food, so the cats would thrive and provide good fishing for the future. It seemed to go against everything we believed in about nature, but it did make sense. And, after all, Jamie did get that snapper out of there for us.

We hauled two plastic garbage bags of catfish fingerlings up to the lake on litters and before turning in that night, tossed a dozen fist-sized poison bombs into the water. This kind of poison goes inert within twenty-four hours of being diluted, so the lake could be stocked before we left.

There is no way to describe the sight that greeted us bright and early the next morning—the stuff nightmares are made of. If there were a thousand little sunfish floating belly side up, there were that many cottonmouth snakes, and probably half as many snapping turtles. I saw probably seven dozen rattlesnakes. Not to mention a million frogs and various other forms of aquatic life. We all stood silently staring at it. By noon it became apparent from the smell that we could not just leave that bloating mass of putrefying flesh to decompose where it was. None of us would ever have entered the water again.

Clean up was accomplished from rickety, leaking handmade canoes with willow switch seines. It took most of the day. I still get nauseated thinking about it. Reeking, slippery, slimy carcasses, some with ivory fangs, others with hard shell beaks, all of them impotent and pitiful in death. We ended the day exhausted and sick at heart. Jamie fell out of favor.

For the next year or so, the water was breached only with the greatest trepidation. How many cottonmouths and snappers had come back? No way to know, but in all the years reservation people have been going up there, no one has ever been assaulted by them. Maybe they never came back, maybe they are giving us a lesson in forgiveness. No one fished there for a whole season to give the cats a chance to grow up and start reproducing. The happy ending to that tale is that ever since then you can pull a big, fat channel cat out of that little lake any time and make a meal of him. We murdered that lake, and in return, it feeds us for generations to come.

SECTION 5:
GOD BLESS AMERICA

THE BAR AT HEART ATTACK AND VINE

This story is a tribute to Tom Waits: quite possibly the greatest poet/wordsmith of our time. While the characters, geography, and events depicted here are original to this author, they are heavily influenced and inspired by the brilliant Tom Waits works Small Change *and* Heart Attack and Vine *(Electra/Asylum Records).*

I t was the kind of dive where the little hairs on the back of your neck stand up as soon as you step through the door, where you know immediately you have stepped into a mistake, but making a U-turn on the threshold would be cowardly, would draw the kind of attention that would make someone want to follow you out.

The subdued rumble was comprised of muffled mumbles, not an air of general gaiety. It was a room of parts, every couple and small group in their own little bubble, although acutely aware of everyone else, every movement and attitude. There were those here, hunched over drinks, apparently oblivious to all else, who could smell who was carrying a gun, who was dangerous without one, and who had been to the Big House. Everyone in this bar had several escape strategies in mind, "just in case." There was no reason to believe anything would erupt—other than that in such a gathering violence is endemic; it is a tangy, metallic sensation on the back of the tongue, a burnt, electrical smell in the air. People in this room would spill blood tonight. Only the details were left to be worked out.

121

The music was raunchy. On a small platform stage, a rumpled refugee from Ginsberg's era was dragging an original tune through a rusty smoke-and-whiskey-cured voice reminiscent of Satchmo.

They drink whiskey. A cigarette ember brightens to reflect eyes that are a bottomless well of black ink; eyes that register, catalog, evaluate, but are windows into nothingness. The men in this room live alone. Some own a female, but none cohabitate. They function on a primitive level, thoughts translating into action without being filtered through troubling theoretical abstractions such as conscience and the finer points of statutory law. They exist on the underside of a society most people are unaware of, where existence is invariably nasty, brutish and short. Everyone in this room, in his or her own time, will die a violent death, a fact of life accepted as inevitable as sunrise and given as much contemplation.

The air in this room is stale, but opening windows and running a fan would not change that. It is a staleness that permeates the woodwork, the glassware, and the people themselves. Cigarette smoke, fear, and broken dreams have been a part of this cave for too long. Nothing short of a holocaust would cleanse it.

Time drags. Money changes hands. Eyes slide and scan. Nobody trusts anybody. Rightfully so. Faces change, the attitude remains the same. Sensors stay alert for any sign of weakness, any momentary waver in defenses.

The few lone women here are unapproachable. They are here because they are shipwrecks, crash landings and fiery debris—not Daddy's Little Princess or last season's Homecoming Queen. Their troubled souls seek the solace of kindred spirits. Communal misery is better than drinking alone. Occasionally, a lone female will come here driven by twisted desires that demand a certain amount of brutality, but always she finds more than is necessary, desired or healthy. None ever comes here twice.

A siren rips the night in half, and a chill ripples across the room. Fresh cigarettes spark to life. Eyes unconsciously shift through a mental checklist.

Down the street a group of battle-hardened detectives mills around a rapidly cooling corpse, sipping cold coffee from styrofoam cups, being careful not to stain their wingtips in the widening pool of congealing blood, laughing at the punchline of a story about some whorehouse in Des

Moines, hoping that the thin blue line holds until they can get out of this crummy neighborhood. None wants to suggest rousting the bar at Heart Attack and Vine, even though procedure would suggest that is the place to start poking around. Instead, they harass the gimpy newsboy thought to have inherited the stiff's velveteen snap brim hat. The old men at The Squire—rooms nitely or weekly—wheeze T.B. into the cloying humid syrup that is the night air. Nobody saw anything and the cops don't care. Roving prostitutes are drawn by the commotion, alert to the signs: who will be good to go after this? Pockets are picked, car doors are tried, and a cop lifts a racing form from the stiff's pocket, making a mental note to put a couple bucks on the picks circled in red. Blood flows in a rivulet down the sidewalk crack to drip over the curb and mix with crankcase oil and the sordid leavings of an army of winos, crack whores, and stray dogs.

The meat wagon finally arrives and two bleary-eyed, stoned-on-Lebanese-hash losers grumble about having to pick up "a soggy one," and they make a show of donning coveralls, face masks and rubber gloves. Inside the wagon, they quickly rifle the pockets for what the cops left behind and argue over how to split three vending machine prophylactics, a five-pack of Swisher Sweets and a broken Timex. They bet five bucks on whether or not he has any jailhouse tattoos and charge a nervous chicken hawk seven bucks for a lift across town. Someone from the city is supposed to come and spray the blood away, but of course he won't. It is soon crawling with flies delighted to leave maggots behind and sewer rats who think they must have pleased the gods mightily to deserve such rich manna. It is criss-crossed with bicycle tire tracks, stroller wheels and footprints, a damp, slippery island of corruption no less wholesome than any other patch of real estate this side of Division Street. This is a universe comprised of that which stains, pools, oozes, and settles on the lowest plateau available. Some stains feed the netherworld; some are parasitic, not imitating life but mocking it.

Across the street from the bar is a pawn shop as tired and dreary as the bag ladies and junkies who come here to trade. They drag in with ill-gotten treasures clasped in greasy fingers, convinced that this time they will not accept peanuts. But of course they do. They add their trinkets to the flotsam of desperate and crippled lives. Yet another enterprise thriving on the refuse of shattered dreams, unopened parachutes and seeds that never

123

blossomed. A way station for the shuffling parade of unwanted, unwashed, and unrecognized who make up this little corner of paradise. The stuttering shoe-shine boy out front moonlights as an axe murderer.

Everything about The Squire's lobby says Old Men Live Here. The odor of flaking scalps, cheap cigars and dreams long abandoned permeates the stuffy, unconditioned air. A worn, tattered No Cooking or Visitors in Rooms sign, older even than most of the inhabitants, is peeling from the yellowing wall behind a battered front desk. A lamp flickers—even the electricity is tired—producing a stroboscopic light show against the freckled pate of the snoozing desk clerk. Obese old men in polyester pants sit in worn, overstuffed chairs repaired with electrical tape and terry cloth scraps, and gaze unwaveringly at nothing; occasionally their lips move but they make no sound. They are losers in a way no young man can be. There is no time left to start over, to convince themselves that their big break is just around the corner, that they are going to meet the woman of their dreams and live happily ever after. It will never get any better than this, and this sucks. It can still get worse and whatever worse is lurks around the next bend. There are no rules here forbidding younger people or women to check in, but it doesn't happen. Any whose circumstances bring them into this lobby do an immediate about-face. The expression they wear on the way out is not a reflection of disgust, but of the uncomfortable feeling that they have glimpsed their own destiny and have arrived here much too soon. There is no rush.

The sounds here are those of phlegmy coughs and labored breathing. Even in the most humid August, this place is dry and brittle; on the freshest spring day, it is musty and drear. The Philosopher once said, "When you got nothin', you got nothin' to lose." The flip side of that is, when you've got almost nothing, that little bit becomes precious. When you have no more than a room at The Squire, a cardboard suitcase and a hot plate, there is very little between you and them bums on the park benches. When a few lousy bucks, like some cheap punk might have in his pockets at any time, is the difference between a roof and Skid Row, that cheap punk would be well-advised to watch himself and avoid wandering into blind alleys.

Tough guys are supposed to have names like Nick or Louie. They are ruggedly handsome and people know automatically not to mess with them. Every once in a great while, one of them will beat all the odds and grow old, develop a big belly and a swollen nose with spiderwebs of burst capillaries. Sometimes he goes from being feared and respected to being a cheap joke, a caricature of his former self.

Harold sat at the bar, nursing his drink and grumbling under his breath. He grumbled because it had become his nature, but inside, Harold was a happy man. For this moment he could relive his glory days, when the dames hung on him and he got the respect he deserved. The whiskey, this room, these people—everything here brought that back vividly.

The jigger of Black Velvet seared a patch down his throat like white heat across the tundra. An agony and an ecstasy in a shot. He closed his eyes and braced himself to minimize any outward display. It had been too long. But there was a time . . . boy, was there a time. Now it had come to this. The snubnose .38 in his pants pocket pressed against his thigh like a lover's caress. Even though he wasn't the old Harold, that blue steel made him equal to the toughest wise guy in this bar and the captain of his own ship.

The bar at Heart Attack and Vine serves liquor until sun-up. At the first suggestion of a pale, watery luminescence over the top of the brick factory a block away, the barkeep announces closing time. "You don't have to go home, but you can't stay here," he deadpans for the one millionth time. The occasion goes unremarked. The room stirs. This is the time they all secretly dread. The despised Ra is about to expose more than can be comfortably revealed, to light up dark corners, cast shadows and bring to life that part of the world best avoided. It is time when solitude must be faced—to curl up alone at the mercy of the demons in one's head, or damp them down with pills or booze. It is time to make sure doors are locked, a loaded pistol is under the pillow and there are no monsters lurking under the bed. It is time to wind down another twenty-four hour period of existence and simultaneously look forward to and dread the next.

Harold was walking on marshmallows, chuckling over some long-forgotten conquest, working his way toward The Squire when his world was transformed into a stunning bright light. After the momentary shock of the spotlight, the megaphone voice that commanded him to put his hands on top of his head and face the wall was no surprise. So this is where it ends, he thought. No regrets.

The stubby had barely left his pocket when a million angry bits of white-hot lead reduced Harold to hamburger on the corner of Heart Attack and Vine.

For the second time since midnight, the coroner's office dispatched their stoned, grumbling EMS techs to the neighborhood to remove all evidence of man's latest inhumanity to man. This time the rookie cop told them the one about the whorehouse in Des Moines and was rewarded with a toke from their hash pipe. Police ballistics experts were soon to be amazed at how many samples they had on file that matched the antique taken from the no-name fat guy who drew down on the homicide squad and went out in a blaze.

Across the street, a tired, washed-out whore watched Harold's exit without flinching. "Harold has fallen and he can't get up," she said in a bitter, mimicky voice. She took a long drag on a bent Pall Mall and flicked it at a passing motorist. "Sap," she muttered. Doris was as grey and hard as the granite wall she stood before. The law of the jungle prevailed here, and Doris was a survivor. She had no patience with weakness. Suicide was for the weak. Doris knew that when her time came, she would go out fighting and take a couple of those sonsabitches with her. Harold was a sap.

Doris was past her prime. Had been for a long time. These days she subsisted on that part of the freak trade she thought of as the "mommy biz." Always an innovator, Doris had found her niche under that rock where she seemed to look like every sicko's mother, grandmother, piano teacher or babysitter. After a lifetime in the business, she liked to think there were no surprises left. There were. Doris could be surprised, but not amazed—never shocked. Surprises were shrugged off. Watching a has-been who had once been a subject of respect reenact the final scene from Bonnie and Clyde or learning yet another twisted kink in the endless circus that is human sexuality aroused no more than a shrug. She knew enough about freaks to know that massive bloodletting twice in one night would bring them out in droves.

The door to Harold's room on the third floor of The Squire imploded with a loud bark and the weasel-faced scavenger that had pushed it in rushed to the corner, snatched the hot plate there and quickly retreated. He wanted to scrounge for other treasure, but left that to the more timid rodents who would scurry in on his heels; this act of boldness had completely exhausted his limited supply of testosterone. It was a pair of very rubbery knees that carried him to his own grimy den and threatened to buckle at every step. He immediately plugged in his prize and set a can of generic pork and beans on the coil. Broken, dirt-caked fingernails brushed through his scant hair as he licked his lips in anticipation. Harold had once told him he had enough film on his teeth to shoot Lawrence of Arabia and the newsreel. He didn't get exactly what that meant, but he hated Harold for it. He chortled over his victory: not only did he get to watch Harold go out like a sucker, his standard of living limped up a notch at the same time. "Screw you, Harold," he whispered aloud, drool sliming his stubbled chin. After several long minutes of staring stupidly at the cold ring before him, a quiet, barely perceptible rattle coughed to life in the barren wasteland inside his skull. It grew to a recognizable laugh, growing until it filled the room. "Screw you, Mucus Mouth." The hot plate didn't work.

Doris made her way to the second floor walk-up she called Home Sweet Home as much by pulling on the handrail as by putting one foot ahead of the other. It has turned out to be an exhausting morning. Not surprisingly, there were a few surprises.

A curved, well-enameled fingernail scooped a pinch of China white heroin to Doris's nose, where it disappeared in a whiff. A visitor to this paradise for decades, she had the reserve to space the indulgence out enough to keep that wretched monkey off her back. "You'll never get that lucky," she says aloud to nobody.

Doris is not the storybook hooker with a heart of gold. She did not study real estate in the evenings or have grand aspirations of moving on to bigger and better. The fantasy of a home in the suburbs, children and a station wagon with wood on the side is as foreign to her as screen doors to a shellfish. Doris is a realist and a thinker. She has lived longer and better than anyone she was young with. "Because I am smarter than all of them put together, is why," she often reminds herself. Doris is smart enough to not let anyone get too close, to know when to get out. Doris is gifted with the innate ability to look into anyone's eyes and know if they were to be avoided. Her most important survival skill is the ability to retrieve and swing a straight razor with a speed and accuracy a king cobra would envy. If there were such a thing as ballistics examinations on razor blades, the cold steel folded and tucked under her left garter would be of enormous interest to the boys downtown.

A curled, yellowing Kodak print depicting a debonair young wiseguy in a snazzy three piece suit and smartly cocked Stetson hat with one arm around the belle of the ball was wedged into the mirror over her bureau. "Goodbye, sap," she said, plucking the print and dropping it into the wastebasket.

As Doris floats dreamily above it all, serenaded by Count Basie's orchestra, a faded, watery sun is drawn reluctantly across a drab, leaden sky, peeking morosely over the rooftops into the neighborhood of Heart Attack and Vine. It radiates nothing cheerier than a bleak, stingy luminescence which, while not darkness, cannot in good conscience be referred to as daylight. It shines down, not on an idyllic burg with laughing children, yipping dogs and dreamy lovers, but a sullen and desolate moonscape of life's walking wounded. Grass refuses to grow here; nowhere does a bird sing or cricket chirp. Early morning scavengers shuffle through alleys, checking behind dumpsters and parked cars for pockets that have not been rifled, doors left unlocked, and bottles with a slug left in the bottom.

While other parts of town are coming to life and starting to bustle, this one is in its dormant state. Its inhabitants have withdrawn to regroup, to unwind, to lick their wounds. They remain invisible to that world outside of their bubble, a world that has no clue what roams the night while they sleep, and is better off for that blissful ignorance. Those who live here only come out at night. In former lives they lurked in the darkest corners of the deepest caves, or under the skin of a rotting carcass. They come and go unannounced. No one leaves a forwarding address or is missed when they are gone.

GOD BLESS AMERICA:
THE SAGA OF AN AMERICAN SOCIAL CLIMBER

I t is an hour before dawn on the two block stretch of Second Street where those seeking day work congregate every morning. A pickup slows to the curb and a dozen hopefuls run over to it. A deal is quickly struck and several pile in the back, a scene that will be repeated a number of times this morning but enough to satisfy only a small percentage of those looking to earn a day's pay.

Many of those here are just going through the motions: alcoholism, mental illness, drug addiction, or terminal laziness prohibit any employment beyond panhandling. They are here because the Salvation Army turns them out at five a.m., or because the dumpsters or other nooks they sleep in are about to be disturbed by the new day's commerce. For them, this is a place to be, to have peers, to not be looked down upon and scorned. It is a place to pick up news that is relevant to their world, to form alliances for the day of begging and shoplifting that lies ahead.

For others, it is a chance to get a toe-hold. To get on a construction crew for the day and show some employer what hard workers they are and snag a real job. It is at least a chance to get some work, to earn enough for a meal, maybe a room somewhere, to get through another day with some modicum of dignity until a real break comes along. A man who really wants to can find a way to get on his feet down here on Second Street.

129

Nobody knew much about the Hustler, but that was not uncommon. This was a subculture that discouraged a lot of personal questions. Those whose histories made them sensitive to the signs assumed that he had done hard time somewhere but that, too, was unremarkable. People came and went; some had more substance than was apparent at first glance, some were as vacuous as they appeared. Most were too involved in their own little worlds to be concerned about those around them or were too dull to be curious.

He never gave anyone a name, but after he showed up about five-thirty one morning with a gym bag slung over his shoulder, the tag "Hustler" was automatically applied. Some of the regulars thought he had been around for a couple weeks, catching work when he could, but it wasn't until this one particular morning that they paid any attention. The first time someone tried to bum a cigarette, this guy zipped open his bag and pulled out a little package which turned out to contain some Bugler cigarette tobacco and eight rolling papers. Enough for five really good cigarettes or eight "skinny Minnies." Twenty-five cents, one of those half-sized books of matches included. This created a stir. A dozen packs were sold in a matter of minutes. Those with some change, but not enough, started seeking each other out to go halves on a pack. The Hustler was hard-nosed that first week. Don't even bother asking if he will take twenty-four cents. As the days went on and everyone knew him and eagerly anticipated his arrival each morning, sales skyrocketed to where he was buying Bugler by the case a couple times a week.

One day he found a coupon for fifty percent off with the purchase of two packages of sliced salami, and another for three loaves of generic white bread for a dollar. Those purchases in hand, along with pockets full of mustard packages swiped from a hot dog vendor, he quadrupled his investment in ten minutes selling sandwiches to the afternoon crowd under the Drake Bridge downtown. Sometimes he would trade a twenty-five cent item for a fifty cent welfare bus voucher and go up on the far north end of town to a shop that sold day-old donuts really cheap. Sometimes they would let him get all of their two-day-olds for almost nothing. These were individually priced down on Second, ranging from five cents to two for a quarter.

Different products came out of that shoulder bag at different times, depending on availability, but always priced within reach of those to whom the penny and nickel are still significant monetary units. He knew all the hangouts and showed up at various times during the day, always with that bag of things to sell. He was often seen sitting in the shade sipping an iced tea across from everyone's favorite begging spot near the UT campus. Quite often he would spread out a beach towel to display to passing students the craft items he made for sale. Throughout the afternoon, the regulars would take him their humble proceeds and make their purchases. It was widely speculated that he made more money drinking iced tea than most of them could make at day labor. They were alternately fascinated, envious, and resentful. Some wondered aloud what kind of connections this guy had. Some were convinced he was a cop. Many decided they would do the same thing, although such resolve is hard to maintain. The cheapest bottle of wine costs three dollars, and it takes most of the day to scrounge that up. A can of Bugler is five dollars and some change. Out of reach. There were a number of mugging conspiracies contemplated, but the Hustler never seemed to be drunk, appeared to be pretty healthy, and he was always so damned *alert*.

None of them realized he had spent his first days in town in the hobo jungle on Town Lake (the stretch of the Colorado River that bisects downtown), just behind the newspaper office, although he recognized a number of them. In those days, he would rise early, bathe in the river, shave in a piece of rear-view mirror tied to a tree and, after breakfast at the Sally Ann, go out in search of opportunity. He had learned that neatness counts, and that an English-speaking person willing to work hard in exchange for cash and not a lot of questions can usually find something. His first break came before the second month was out: three days' work for a landscaper who wanted someone to live on the premises to protect his stock at night. It didn't take long to work out an agreement. Benefits included a Chevy van set on blocks with a bed already built in, roomy enough for his carefully selected yard sale wardrobe and electricity for his AM/FM radio, as well as a key to the service station restroom next door. Who could ask for more? The real beauty was having an actual address, which opened the door to securing a driver's license. During his hippie days he had learned the art of sliding into motel rooms between the time the patrons left and the maids arrived to shower, use the phone, procure complimentary soap, shampoo, and razors, as well as take advantage of the free continental breakfast. The Howard Johnson's two blocks from his new home was a Godsend.

The last time any of the Second Street crowd saw the Hustler was when he showed up down at the jungle carrying an enormous keg of beer. He filled up sixteen-ounce bottles (bring your own) for thirty-five cents and realized a one thousand percent return on his investment.

Nobody paid any particular attention a couple days after that as Yellow Cab #47 cruised by that corner of Second, and chances are if they had noticed, it wouldn't have registered who the driver was.

Two years later, a newly purchased pickup turns onto Second Street and pulls to the curb. The driver tells a couple of raggedy but reasonably sober-looking hopefuls that he needs some help loading a moving van. He offers more than the going rate and swings through the downtown McDonald's to get them breakfast on the way.

He figures these boys will need their strength: he has rented the largest van available and has a lot of stuff to move out to the piece of land he has just bought out in the Hill Country. Thinking about it, he chuckles. "Only in America," he says out loud.

Additional copies of *God Bless America: Stories by Some Guy in the Joint* may be ordered by sending $13.00 check or money order to:

The Phillip Lippert Defense Fund
P.O. Box 132
Adrian, Michigan 49221

Donations may also be sent to this address.

For updates on the author's legal progress, visit the website of the Phillip Lippert Defense Fund at <www.Phillip-Lippert.com>. This website was created and is maintained by Lippert's supporters; the State of Michigan does not provide computers or internet access to prisoners.